In an unexpe
swing by the cha
backward, with n ... between
them. All at once Kiara went dizzy and hyper-focused, tempted once more by that full, supple mouth, and the satiny-looking fall of his thick brown hair as he leaned over her. He was close enough to touch. In this moment, she wanted nothing more than to do just that.

"Some time, at some point, I'd like to hear more about that, Kiara. I'd like very much to know how you became the woman you are."

She looked at him steadily. "I'd bore you to tears. It's nothing extraordinary."

"All present evidence to the contrary." He set her gliding once again and Kiara's stomach performed a sparkling fall-away. She delighted in his words but forced herself to brush them aside before they could take root and sway her into believing he saw richness to her spirit. After all, it was part of Ken's persona to be gracious and encouraging.

But he continued, and those arguments splintered to shards when he said, "You're moving forward in directions that are not only admirable, but eye-opening—not just for you, most likely, but to everyone who's part of your life—don't hold to what other people see, or expect of you. Be who you are. And while you're at it, create the best version of yourself you can imagine. The only question, with the only relevance that matters, is this, Kiara: Who are you *now*?"

Hearts Surrender

by

Marianne Evans

This is a work of fiction. Names, characters, places, and incidents either are the product of the author's imagination or are used fictitiously, and any resemblance to actual persons living or dead, business establishments, events, or locales, is entirely coincidental.

Hearts Surrender
  Woodland Series, Book 2

        Contact Information: titleadmin@whiterosepublishing.com

Cover Art by *Nicola Martinez*

White Rose Publishing,
a division of Pelican Ventures, LLC
www.whiterosepublishing.com
PO Box 1738 *Aztec, NM * 87410

Publishing History
First White Rose Edition, 2010
Library of Congress Control Number: 2010933682
Print Edition ISBN 978-0-9842968-2-8
eBook Edition ISBN 978-0-9842968-3-5
Published in the United States of America

Dedication

To my church family at Guardian Angels. You're an inspiration to me in so many ways - and an ever-present reminder of God's community of love. Thank you for the blessing of your friendship and faith life. To Denise Ficorelli in particular, thanks for your help with the mission trip information and research questions. The youth of Guardian Angels are so blessed by your service!

Praise for Hearts Crossing

Evans presented a plot that was impressive. I loved the way this book unfolded. It showed a realistic look at Christians without being preachy or over-the-top. I know anyone who reads this book will love it. In fact, I hope there is a sequel.

~5-Hearts , The Romance Studio

Ms. Evans knows how to set a scene. Her word descriptions put you right there until you can taste the scented breeze....It's a story which touches the heart and tickles the senses.

~4.5 Books, LASR

Hearts Crossing is a perfect example of why I love Inspirational romance: ...Beautiful writing and characters you won't soon forget.

~Award Winning Author, Cindy K. Green

Both Daveny and Collin are wonderful characters who have a delightful relationship. I enjoyed the path to Collin's returning faith and the sweetness of Hearts Crossing.

~4.5 Books – Top Pick/ Night Owl Reviews

...Hearts Crossing offers a wonderful reminder of the personal renewal and revitalization that is possible with God and I am looking forward to reading more from this author in the near future!

~4.5 Clovers / Crystal, Kwips & Kritiques

1

Kenneth Lucerne donned a weighty, calf-length vestment, the white, gold-trimmed mantle of his calling. In the seclusion of his pastoral office at Woodland Church, he adjusted its fit and fall.

Something in his spirit tried to ignite...and failed.

A centering breath later, he closed his eyes, and prayed. *God, grace me with the strength to fulfill the mission You have entrusted to my care. Grant me the heart and wisdom to share Your mercy, Your love, and Your truth. Please be with me, in Jesus' name. Amen.*

Beyond the partially-opened door came the gradually building noise from the narthex as parishioners arrived for ten o'clock services.

Ken opened his eyes slowly, seeing and absorbing. First thing that hit him? Naturally, it was the brass framed photograph of his wife, Barb. He firmed his heart against a familiar onslaught of pain as his thoughts performed an auto correct: His *late* wife, Barb.

Outside the office, Ken heard the Edwards family arrive. Their voices stood out—won his interest by virtue of familiarity and deep affection. Exuberant conversations and laughter, so typical to the clan, were interrupted suddenly by the sharp, plaintive cry of a baby. A unison chorus of tender assurances followed, so too, a smattering of gentle coos.

A smile tugged against the corners of his mouth.

Today, Woodland would welcome in baptism the soul of two-month-old Jeffrey Lance Edwards, son of Collin and Daveny Edwards.

He attempted spiritual ignition once again and came closer this time.

Still, a void yawned before him, widened by the prospect of a loving family gathering. Moments like this intensified that deep, almost breath-stealing sense of loss, but he tried not to dwell on that fact. He couldn't afford to think of Barb, of losing the most precious person in his life. Not in a moment so full of God's joy and light.

Determination rode in, heightening his resolve to leave melancholy behind and meet God's present moment head-on, in his role as Pastor.

His heart's ignition switch flickered, sparked hot, and then fired to life.

Leaving the office, he walked a short corridor leading to the church proper.

"Have you ever seen such a perfectly shaped mouth in your *life*?" Collin Edwards asked the family assemblage.

Stepping up from behind, Ken stifled a laugh. Collin fit the stereotypical role of proud father to a 'T', but the emotion behind his comment was authentic and warming.

"Yes, I have," said Collin's wife, Daveny. "Every time I look at you."

Amidst laughter, and a few groans from Collin's brothers, Ken entered the circle of the Edwards family and clapped a hand against Collin's shoulder. "Have you ever seen such a proud *father* in your life?"

Through the enthusiastic welcome he received, through the teasing that ensued, Ken searched...and found. *Kiara Jordan.*

He knew she'd be front and center. Daveny's best friend and business partner wasn't part of the Edwards family by blood, but rather by unanimous consent.

She gently lifted Jeffrey from Daveny's arms and brought the baby into a close tuck. She nuzzled his plump, pink cheek. The fall of Kiara's straight, honey-colored hair danced like a curtain around her shoulders, the satin of which Ken could nearly feel. For a moment, he just stared, taking his fill of a beautiful woman cradling an innocent baby.

"He is, without question, the *cutest* baby *ever*," Kiara said.

"Absolutely," concurred Elise Edwards, the equally proud grandmother.

Ken noticed the somewhat aged christening blanket draped over Kiara's arm. She would be up front with the whole family during the baptism, standing next to the gray and white marble font during the ceremony. Made sense. Daveny Montgomery Edwards, an only child, considered Kiara a surrogate sister.

"You want to see Pastor Ken, Jeffrey?" Kiara murmured, stepping close. She focused her gaze on his, her emerald eyes alive and sparkling. When she handed Jeffrey over, the light scent of a floral perfume drifted up. Like the woman who wore it, the aroma was evocative.

"How are you?" Ken asked quietly, unwilling to relinquish her gaze.

"Good. I'm sure glad to see *you* again. Welcome back." Her smile bloomed, large and beautiful—engaging. It took a few seconds for Ken to find his equilibrium.

"Thanks. It's good to be back."

"How was the mission trip?"

While Ken cuddled Jeffrey, Kiara rubbed the baby's back. The motion left him keenly aware of the connection between the three of them. "It was hard work—but very rewarding."

"You were in Louisiana, right? Just outside of New Orleans? Habitat for Humanity?"

"Exactly." The knowledge that this compelling woman had tracked his absence sent pleasure seeping through his bloodstream. Within her observations, though, Ken sensed an underlying current, one that traveled beyond simple interest. She cared about the answer. So he elaborated. "There's a world of great work being done down there. We helped build new houses, even assisted in improving dilapidated structures inside and out. We fed masses of homeless people, too. In fact, the whole program left me wanting to get members of our youth group motivated to donate some time and muscle to a mission trip of our own—maybe sometime this fall."

Jeffrey's back rub ended when Kiara went still, though her hand remained in place while she looked into Ken's eyes. Almost instantly, the baby started a restless squirm. "Really? What an amazing experience that would be." She retreated a bit, breaking the connection to Jeffrey. She looked down as she ran her fingertips against the tassels that edged the christening blanket. She looked up once more. "You must have enjoyed being a source of help and benefit. I give you a lot of credit."

Ken could tell her comment didn't stem from polite conversation or small talk. Images from the trip came to him, click-by-click, like a slideshow display.

He had witnessed helplessness, poverty, the destitute living conditions of over-burdened families. But he had also witnessed transformation—hope and rebirth delivered by hard working hands and giving hearts.

Giving hearts like Kiara's.

Not for the first time in the years since they had met, Ken sensed within her a quest, a longing for self-discovery. Trouble was, she fought that instinct, too.

So he challenged. "Maybe you can find out." He studied her for a moment. "I have a good memory. I'll remember this conversation if we end up putting the mission trip together. You may become one of my first adult recruits."

She blushed, looking away shyly while she shook her head. Her pattern, he knew, might be to step aside, but her heart turned her toward service—service that could be put to miraculous use.

Magnetized, Ken could have studied her features, that delicate flush of reaction, for much longer; however, family conversations, plans and questions took her away from his direct focus. Besides, more and more parishioners filtered in, sweeping him into his role as Pastor.

Ken tried not to be blatant about watching Kiara, but following their conversation, he had time to consider the ideas he had about crafting a mission trip that involved Woodland Church. In fact, the seeds of that plan took root and bloomed into a flare of color and life that was instantaneous. While he watched her move through the church, mixing with people and chatting, Ken knew he wanted Kiara involved—and he felt confident he could convince her to participate.

That fact alone provided a spurring push of motivation.

2

Even before they met in the common area of Woodland Church, Kiara knew Pastor Ken was back in town, following a month-long sabbatical to participate in a Christian outreach and mission program.

He'd been doing such things a lot during the past couple years—ever since his wife Barb passed away. He had spent weeks in the far reaches of Michigan's upper peninsula working with impoverished families and assisting their far-removed charitable organizations. During the winter months, he had spent countless hours at homeless shelters and soup kitchens around metro Detroit.

This past excursion had been his longest yet, however—a full month away from Woodland. Associate Pastor Ben McCallum always performed admirably, but the heart of Woodland Church beat strongest within the soul of its Pastor, Kenneth Lucerne. For almost a dozen years now—ever since his ordination, according to Daveny—Woodland was his home. Kiara often wondered if that wasn't the reason why in recent times being at the helm of the church seemed difficult for him. After all, at thirty-five, he was far too young to have suffered through the terrible life-quake of becoming a widower.

Despite it all, Kiara gave him tremendous credit for natural charisma, and nothing lessened the impact of being in his presence once again.

Short brown hair, softly waved, framed a face that featured a strong, squared jaw and a pair of warm brown eyes that searched the faces of today's attendees, drawing them in one by one as he preached.

Kiara included.

Before she knew it, his gaze tagged hers. A slight quirk of his lips let her know she'd been busted for staring.

"Where there's love, there is self-sacrifice," Ken said, walking the length of the front line of pews. Kiara shook free of distraction and listened. "There's a giving over, one to the other. A surrender. By that I don't just mean the surrender of time, or of giving up a few hours...right now probably *more* than a few hours...of sleep to soothe the cries of a newborn baby." Ken smiled at Daveny and Collin who sat next to her. He slid his hand tenderly against Jeffrey's cheek. "What I mean by surrender is sacrifice. Love can't grow into place without self-surrender. If either withholds the self, love cannot exist."

Ken continued. "You know what? Sacrifice gets a bad rap. Sacrifice evokes the image and emotion of denial, of setting aside something we wish for. That's not the case here. When we speak of sacrifice in this instance, it involves nurturing and seeing to the needs of a newborn, sometimes as we set aside our own wants and needs. It's selfless. We give and teach as a baby becomes a toddler, and yet again, as that child grows to adulthood beneath the protective wings of a loving parent and family. Furthermore, those sacrifices aren't without benefit. For example? What a blessing, to witness the good that comes from watching a newborn grow into a self-sufficient being who remains, always, a part of our hearts and lives. Ultimately though, our children reach independence. When that happens, a different kind of surrender takes place. A release of the ones we love to the fullness of life—knowing in our hearts that the unchanging truth of God's ultimate shepherding always stays in place."

The sermon concluded a short time later, and Ken invited the Edwards family to gather around a baptismal font stationed to the right of the altar. Kiara followed behind Daveny. Once everyone was in place, Jeffrey's christening blanket was removed. Then, clothed only in a cloth diaper, he was handed to Pastor Ken.

Ken offered introductory blessings and a prayer before holding him over the warmed, gurgling water of the font. "Jeffrey Lance Edwards, the Christian community of Woodland welcomes you with great joy. I baptize you in the name of the Father, and of the Son, and of the Holy Spirit. Amen."

As he spoke, Pastor Ken dipped Jeffrey into the water three times. The family gathered in close and a few flashes went off, recording the moment. Swaddling Jeffrey in fresh, white linen adorned by a vivid red cross, and lifting the baby carefully, Pastor Ken walked the main aisle of the church in a ceremonious presentation to the parish of its newest member. Chills of pure joy skimmed against Kiara's skin as piano music swelled and the congregation chimed in with a sung chorus of "Alleluia."

Tears filled her eyes and spilled slowly down her cheeks. She looked over at Daveny, who watched the proceedings and glowed with happiness; her eyes sparkled with moisture as well and Collin tucked his arm around her waist, drawing her tight to his side.

They both looked so proud, so fulfilled. Kiara rejoiced deeply for her dearest friends and their newborn son—named in part for Collin's late brother.

When Ken returned to the baptismal font, he handed Jeffrey to Daveny, but his gaze settled on Kiara's at the moment a fresh trickle of tears fell free. She dashed them away fast. It was time to leave services temporarily so that Jeffrey could be dressed in his baptismal garments.

Before returning to the proceedings, however, Ken passed by and discreetly pressed an item into her right hand. A soft, snow-white handkerchief. He touched her with a smile that made her muscles go weak.

❧❦

Seeking a few moments of peaceful meditation following services, Kiara ducked back into the church. It would take a while for the crowds to thin, for the Edwards family to accept the multitude of congratulations and admiring comments.

The idea prompted a smile and a sense of contentment on behalf of her friends. Daveny and Collin could make even the most jaded person believe in the power of love all over again.

Which became part of Kiara's quandary at the moment.

She longed to taste that kind of happiness, but trying to find it always seemed to end her up in tight, complex emotional tangles. Like the situation she faced right now with her most current male admirer…

"You coming, Kiara?"

The summons startled her. Kiara turned when she felt Daveny's hand come to rest on her shoulder. She hadn't even heard her friend approach—testimony to the degree of distraction she fought. "Yeah, I am. Sorry."

"No worries, sweetie. Just wondered about you is all." Daveny sat next to her with a sigh. "OK, so the pudgy ankles are gone, the waistline is starting to resemble that of a normal human being again, but I'm here to tell you; Ken wasn't kidding. *Boy,* does sleep deprivation take it out of you."

Kiara grinned. "I slept in until eight thirty this morning."

"Wench."

"Stop snarling. I may have slept through the night, but I don't have a beautiful baby boy to tend to. And I certainly didn't wake up next to a man the likes of Collin Edwards."

"Was it Andrew, perhaps?" Daveny asked tentatively.

"No." The reply was flat and lifeless.

Daveny paused. "Have you decided?"

On the inside, Kiara cringed. On the inside, she braced against…everything. Right versus wrong. God versus the devil in her soul.

In an instant, Kiara found herself thousands of miles away. She traversed the narrow, cobbled streets of Paris, hand in hand with a sexy, and admittedly, besotted suitor, her world painted a soft, dusky shade of rose. In her mind's eye, she saw the Eiffel Tower framed in the window of a five-star hotel where she lounged on a balcony overlooking the ancient, gorgeous city. She could almost feel a cool evening breeze ripple the glossy fabric of a satin robe and negligee against her skin.

Beyond the set of double French doors at her back?

Andrew—dark haired, olive skinned, a bewitching specimen—stretched out upon a king-sized bed, tangled up in its sheets, half covered by a plush down comforter...

"Kiara?"

Jarred back to reality by Daveny's voice, Kiara took a deep breath and spoke from the heart. "I realize my 'No' should be automatic. It's wrong. His offer to take me to France for a romantic getaway feels too much like a deliberate ploy. A blatant seduction. Payment for services rendered."

Daveny didn't agree, or disagree. But then, she didn't need to. Like a good friend, she waited and allowed Kiara to come to terms.

"Why does it appeal to me so strongly?" Kiara wondered aloud. "Why is it so hard to just refuse and move on?"

"Because he's attractive. He's successful, and he's absolutely enchanted by you, Kiara. He has been from the start of our landscaping project for his company. He's offering you a trip that's certainly a fantasy come true. Once in a lifetime."

Daveny was correct. First class flight, the Ritz Hotel, a week of...

Surrender to mutual attraction.

But was it mutual? Was it *right*?

Kiara studied the simple altar illuminated by vibrant stained glass windows that framed its perimeter. She wondered. Did her longing to agree to this trip stem from feelings she harbored for Andrew, or from the fact that she felt increasingly lonely? After all, what woman wouldn't enjoy being sought after by a well-to-do, sexy man who wanted to treat her like a princess?

"However," Daveny continued, "let me be clear about something. When all is said and done? You deserve *much* more than a seductive interlude, Kiara. You deserve a man, a relationship, of substance and honor. Don't lose sight of that. Is this developing relationship playing to your heart? Do you really even know him?"

Kiara shrugged. "Well, that's kind of the point. To escape together, to find our footing—"

"Really?"

Kiara heard and understood the skeptical tone—and found no fault with the mild reprimand that rode beneath its surface. "Well, no. It's about…well—"

Chuckling wryly, Daveny bumped Kiara's shoulder with hers. "I know, I know."

A frail sense of self, a near life-long quest for affirmation, clawed at Kiara's chest. By careful design, that fact might surprise most people who knew her. She wore a Donna Karan ensemble from Saks, a new pair of Jimmy Choos. Perfectly styled hair and an expert application of makeup downplayed every flaw and up-played every attribute like a protective shield. Her smile lit up, her bubbly personality engaged…

But the demons she fought were over 25-years-old, and they were relentless.

She stood and sighed through the smile. "I'm going to say no. I know you're right. I know I deserve more, I know what God would want, but so far, the best offers I get come from men who are attracted to this face, this figure, and not much more. To be honest, I've played to that truth for so long, I'm not so sure about finding a way out." She shrugged. "Trapped in my own cage, I guess."

Daveny watched her for a few moments then took

her hand in a firm squeeze. "Don't *ever* sell yourself short like that, Kiara. You're anything but shallow—or immoral. You'll find the one—the one who will give you so much more than you've gotten so far. God's preparing you, honey. And when you're ready, I promise, He'll send you a man who looks deep and long at *who* you are, not just the gorgeous cover-work."

Too serious. Too close to home. Kiara forced herself into an easy-going demeanor, re-sealing her heart as they left the serenity of the church. She tossed Daveny a saucy look, and then linked their arms together. "By the time that happens, I'll be ninety-something, but hope does indeed spring eternal. Come on. The family's waiting."

In the narthex, Pastor Ken stood amidst the Edwards family, temporary custodian of Jeffrey, who gurgled and squiggled. A cloth had been draped over Ken's shoulder to protect his vestment. He cuddled Jeffrey against it and rubbed the infant's back, swaying just a bit, in time to music only the two of them could hear. Kiara's forward progress halted while she absorbed more of the scene—his soft, assuring hum of sound, the tender way he held Jeffrey close.

Thoughts of Andrew left her empty. Instead, she made a wish, then and there, that a man who possessed the tenderness and charisma of Ken Lucerne might be out there for her...somewhere.

3

Early summer breezes set pastel-hued tablecloths rippling. Contentment filled Ken as he absorbed the musk of flowers and the spice of cooking meat that flavored the air. A dozen or so picnic tables filled the space of Daveny and Collin's backyard. Inside their house, he passed through the kitchen where clusters of friends and family bustled, preparing the fixings for brunch following Jeffrey's baptism.

"Hey, Pastor Ken," Kiara called when he walked by. "Can you please grab that platter of biscuits? The one right there next to the stove?"

"Sure."

Flushed and in her glory, Kiara hoisted pitchers of lemonade and water from inside the refrigerator and made ready to return to the backyard. He followed, carrying the requested tray.

"Hey, Kiara?"

"Um-hm?" She turned and her hair slid against her shoulders and shimmered in a way that tantalized his senses.

"Let me promise you something."

"What's that?" Already she grinned, seeming to decipher the mischievous tone of his voice.

He lowered his voice to a whisper and leaned close. "God won't stir up an earthquake or a volcano or anything if you should happen to call me *Ken*."

The pink tinge on her cheeks intensified. He moved by her with a wink, delighted at catching her off guard.

"What about Kenny?" she sassed right back. "Will that suffice?"

He laughed at the rejoinder while they continued through the yard and placed their items on the food table. "Not if you expect to live to tell about it."

"Spoken like a true man of God, *Ken*." Kiara turned back toward the house. Before leaving, she cast a deliberate look over her shoulder and delivered a playful grin.

He watched her disappear inside, enjoying how easily they fell into affectionate teasing. At the heart of the matter, though, he wanted and hoped for her to think of him in terms that weren't strictly related to his role as a pastor. Of late, despite an abundance of people in his life, he felt desperately short of friends and the intimate tapestry of close relationships. Marriage to Barb had helped insulate him from the sensation of being isolated and somehow set apart from the world-at-large. Now, as a widowed pastor, rules and perceptions had definitely changed.

He lingered at the table and a short time later Kiara returned, this time carrying a large platter of fluffy scrambled eggs. Ken decided to go back to the house as well, wanting to see what else might be needed. When she smiled in passing, when their shoulders brushed, warmth bloomed outward from his midsection.

Before long, the table overflowed with food. Fragrant bacon and sausage links were left to warm on an electric tray. French toast and a towering stack of pancakes had been added to the mix as well. Ken delivered plates and cutlery, wanting to make a last trip to the kitchen for two carafes of coffee.

All the while, the yard filled with people who arrived for the day's celebration.

That's when he came up short; an unfamiliar man entered the backyard. Kiara moved toward the new arrival, dodging a few colorful balloons that had been tied to the ends of the tables and bobbed in the air.

"Andrew!" she greeted happily, stepping into his offered hug.

"Hey, sweetheart."

He nuzzled her cheek just before they exchanged a quick kiss. Kiara slid her arm through his, giving it a squeeze and sending him one of those smiles that now hit Ken's system like lightening fire.

Meanwhile, Andrew looked left and right, taking in the party scene, shifting in an uncomfortable way while Kiara enthused: "Drew, the ceremony was just *amazing*. It literally left me in tears. Jeffrey was such a good baby, too. He—"

"It's OK that I didn't go, right? I mean, I'm anxious to meet all your friends, but I'm not family after all, and…well…I'm not too comfortable about the whole church thing."

Ken heard Andrew's dismissive words and sank on the inside.

"Give that time. I'm just glad you're here now." Kiara walked him through the maze of tables and people "C'mon. I want you to say hello to Collin and Dav. They've been asking about you."

She led him toward the spot where Daveny and Collin stood. Their conversation faded with distance. A sense of alarm crept through Ken. He centered his attention on the pair and kept it there. He watched as

Andrew's expression softened to congenial, warm lines and he seemed to react kindly to the family. In fact, he seemed to say something that made the group around them laugh merrily. Kiara kept her supportive physical connection in place as they visited for a bit, then wandered toward the display of food.

Don't reject his comments about God's church so easily, Kiara. The thought crashed in, prompting Ken's protective desire to somehow move between them. *Don't compromise the faith-walk you're starting.*

The party progressed and after a time, the celebratory tone of the day displaced all else. He mingled from table to table, enjoying the company of a number of familiar faces from Woodland. He paused from conversations for a moment, stepping over to the food table so he could replenish his mug of coffee. Daveny joined him, linking her arm through his.

"Hello there." She rose on tiptoe to peck his cheek. That made him smile. Ken adored this long-time, spirited member of his congregation. She lived and breathed the spirit of God. With tender love, and leading by example, she had not only won Collin's heart, she had also inspired Collin, once so disillusioned and embattled with God, to return to his faith. "You having fun?"

"I am. You've done a beautiful job, kiddo." With a glance, Ken indicated the festive décor, the tables packed with people that spread across the entirety of their spacious backyard.

"Thanks. I had a ton of help, though. Yours included. Thanks, Ken, for everything you've done. I really feel like Jeffrey became part of God's family today—and you're the conduit."

That analogy Ken couldn't quite accept. "The

community is the conduit. You and Collin are the conduit. Not me."

She shrugged. "OK. Not you alone, but you importantly."

Laughing, he kissed her cheek. "OK, OK. You win. I know better than to argue with a now, likely sleep-deprived, mom."

"You've always been a smart man." She looked around the yard, picking up a celery stick from the vegetable tray and taking a bite. "Have you seen Kiara?"

"Not in the last few minutes. Why?"

"She brought a fruit and cheese tray and I think we should probably bring it out now."

"Yeah, there's actually room for it on the table now," Ken teased, picking up a few stray plates that had been left behind. He stashed them on top of a pair of empty serving platters. "I'll take these in. Let me get the fruit for you."

"Are you sure?"

"Absolutely. Now get back to the party."

Before she could argue, he turned away, retreating to the kitchen. Dishes filled the sink. Paper debris, bows and discarded wrapping paper covered the counter tops and breakfast table. Sunlight streamed in through an oversized window above the sink and silence enveloped and soothed him for a time.

Until he heard voices. A conversation drifted to him from the next room over, the dining room, which adjoined the kitchen via a swinging door.

"So?" This from a male voice he couldn't readily identify.

"So?" That was Kiara.

Her companion—had to be Andrew—chuckled.

"*So* have you decided?"

"Paris."

"Mmmm…Paris."

Ken heard what sounded like a kiss, then Kiara's shy laughter.

His stomach fell away as he realized the implications of their private moment. He felt like a voyeur. He tried not to listen, but their voices carried regardless of his will.

"First class flight," Andrew continued. "Top of the line accommodations; a week of *Europe*, Kiara. Just the two of us. *Imagine it!*"

"I know, I know. It's exotic, and thrilling. Still, something about all of this makes me feel like a kept woman."

Ken heard Andrew sigh.

"Well it shouldn't. This is something I want to do for you." Andrew paused. "You know something? I mean it when I say I've never ever met anyone like you, Kiara. I promise you that. You're all I think about. All I can focus on."

Andrew's voice had softened to velvet. Ken closed his eyes, battling the urge to wince. He wanted to leave. *Knew* he should leave. His feet stayed rooted to the spot.

"Drew—"

"No. *Please.* Hear me out." Silence followed. "I've loved having you work on the landscaping project at my office, but…but…it's over now, and I *hate* that. I want to keep seeing you. I want to *be* with you."

"I've enjoyed it too, but this is so sudden, so fast."

In each syllable of those simple words, Ken heard her longing, her questioning.

Kiara continued. "I…I just…I don't know what to

say to all this. I'm dazzled and amazed, of course, but—but I *can't*!"

"No buts, sweetheart. OK? Yes, you *can*. Just say *yes*. Just trust me. Trust *us*. I want to do this for you. I want you dazzled and amazed, because you dazzle and amaze *me*. Turnabout's fair play, Kiara. I want to take you to one of the most fantastic places in the world, and I don't want you to have to think about a thing except being with me, about where we can go together as a couple—"

"That's just it, Drew. I *have* imagined those things. I've thought about them just as much as you." Her soft, pleading tone dissipated on air that turned muggy with the first signs of an encroaching summer afternoon. Ken felt each notch upward in the temperature with a startling intensity that had nothing at all to do with the weather.

"Don't deny us this chance," Andrew whispered. "I want this so much. I want *you* so much. You and I walking through the streets, hand in hand, kissing under *le Tour Eiffel*—"

"I have to get back to the party," she interrupted, sounding breathless. Even at a distance, Ken detected the underlying desperation in her tone. He went taut against the temptation he knew she faced, trying hard to rebuke it on her behalf.

"Anyway, you're not being fair," she teased. "I can't think straight when you're like this."

"Good. There's nothing wrong with being off balance. Besides, that'd make two of us. This outfit you're wearing is making me crazy. You look gorgeous."

Ken's reaction was instinctive—couldn't be helped. Andrew's comment left him envisioning the way she looked. A white lace skirt edged by blue satin, a sea-blue shell that, in church, had been discreetly covered by a matching cardigan. For the party, the sweater had been removed to reveal dewy soft skin just hinting at the start of a rich, summer tan. Ken pictured the strappy white sandals on her feet, the dancing line of her skirt as it skimmed against her ankles.

And the images didn't just flow; they flooded him. He felt like he had been pulled under by a warm, swift current. Yes, just looking at her, and absorbing her, was plenty enough to intoxicate a man. He couldn't fault Drew for that.

"Thank you for the compliment," she concluded. "Now unhand me, you beast."

"Not...quite...yet."

Ken didn't need to see the kisses they shared. What he heard provided more than enough entrée into the private moment.

"Six short days, Kiara. Think about it. The plane leaves Saturday at 7 p.m. *Please* say you're going to be there."

Ken didn't wait on Kiara's reply. He didn't want to hear it. Nor did he want to intrude any longer. Still, his heart sank. He grabbed the tray filled with cheese and a variety of fruits then headed outside to dodge the possibility of being discovered. Besides, he needed to regain his composure.

But his legs felt like lead.

4

The following Sunday Ken's psyche morphed into radio receiver mode. He prepared for services, yet all the while, he twisted and tuned an internal dial, seeking Kiara, hoping she'd show up and wondering what she chose to do about Andrew's scintillating offer. When she walked through the double doors and entered the narthex, a sense of relief slid so powerfully through his body that it rendered him dissolved. The relief he'd expected, the degree of near euphoria that accompanied, however, took him by surprise.

After church, he found her sitting in the deserted sanctuary, head bowed, hands folded, eyes closed. He couldn't walk away. For a few unobserved moments, he watched her through the etched glass of the main doors to the sanctuary, riveted in place. Reaching forward, he grasped the cool chrome handle and slowly pulled it open.

Quiet footsteps led him to her pew. "Hey, Kiara."

"Hi, Pas...Ken."

He laughed and gave her shoulder a squeeze. "You're getting better." He sat down.

"Old habits and all."

"Am I interrupting?"

"Not at all." She looked at him with an eagerness that reassured. "I'm glad to see you. It's just...well, it's not often I get a chance to absorb the silence and just be still. I sat here, just like this, after the baptism last weekend, and it really helped me find my center."

"Prayer time always does. Really, I don't mean to be rude. I can leave…"

Kiara pondered that statement for a moment, and watched him steadily. "Please don't. It's not so much that I'm even praying; I just take everything in, if that makes any sense." She shrugged shyly and went quiet, as though a bit discomfited by the topic of prayer and her spirit life. Ken, on the other hand, took in her every nuance and revelation.

"For me those are the moments when God speaks loudest," he offered. "Even silence is a prayer."

"Like we're listening instead of monopolizing."

"Exactly. But there's nothing wrong with *petitioning*," he amended. "Either way, I think God just wants us to be with him."

Kiara looked up at him and smiled. His blood pounded thick and heavy.

"I never got a chance to tell you what a beautiful job you did with the baptism." Her eyes went wide and she gasped, cutting off any kind of response he might offer. "Shoot! That reminds me. I forgot your handkerchief at home. I meant to bring it back to you today."

Her chagrin caused him to chuckle. "Don't worry about it." Crazy, yes, but for some reason Ken liked the fact that she had something of his. So instead of dwelling, he switched topics. "Collin's the picture of contentment and pleased fatherhood, isn't he? Plus, over two years after the wedding, I still see Daveny's glow."

Kiara went unusually still, looking toward a large vibrant floral arrangement at the center of the altar.

"They deserve it. They're very special people."

Wistfulness coated her every word. Her tone and posture left Ken more curious than ever as to why she had refused Andrew's extraordinary invitation to jet off to Europe.

"So are you, Kiara."

She shrugged in too dismissive a way.

"I'm glad to see you here today."

"Where else would I…" The words, and her puzzled expression, faded away. She studied him for a long moment, and then her eyes went wide as the broader implication of his comment sank in. Ken regarded her calmly, remaining steady so she could come forward and feel safe about it. "Oh." She blinked. "Oh, my goodness." She enunciated each word and her shoulders drooped beneath a figurative weight. "You *know*? How could you have known…*Daveny*."

"*No*. Daveny would never betray a confidence. I overheard you and your boyfriend talking about Europe. It was at the Christening party. I was in the kitchen getting food. You and Andrew were in the other room talking. I'm sorry. I didn't mean to pry."

Kiara wilted further. She tilted her head back and groaned. "*Great*. To have someone I respect, my Pastor of all people, think of me as a woman of loose morals. That's just *great*."

On the inside Ken froze. *My Pastor. Respect.* Not bad things, to be sure, but those terms defined the parameters of her feelings. Her perceptions. He didn't come away feeling altogether flattered.

He stood in an abrupt motion. "Thanks for the confidence, Kiara. I only brought it up because I thought you might have some faith in my care and friendship." He snapped the words and moved toward the aisle. Her eyes revealed she was stricken. Too bad. Simplicity turned complex with regard to her presence in his life these days.

But then she stopped him with a restraining hand. "I said no to him. Obviously. I'm here. I didn't end up going."

"That's between the two of you," Ken concluded more gently this time. He didn't sit quite yet. He felt raw, his vulnerabilities exposed.

"I'm so sorry," she whispered. She sounded miserable. He sat, and let her continue. "I'm so sorry you heard that conversation, and I'm sorrier still for what you must think of me because of it."

Once more with what other people thought. Ken wanted to cringe. "Does the opinion of others matter that much to you, Kiara?" He sighed, agonized over an onrush of want. He'd always admired her tender, energetic spirit. Now, however, he had no idea what to do with a desire that intensified each time he saw her. "Let me assure you. I'm nobody's judge. That's not what I'm about, and judgment is certainly not part of my job description."

"I didn't mean it that way! Still, I can't help caring about what you think. I value your opinion because I care about *you*."

The admission stopped him short, flowed against his unsettled heart like a softly curving breeze. "So you want to know what *I* think?"

She nodded. Her eyes remained turbulent, though.

He gathered in a breath, ached to reach for her hands, which still lay folded in her lap. He couldn't cross that physical line right now though, so he held back. "I think you displayed a lot of fortitude and strength turning down what must have seemed like a wonderful opportunity. Fortunately, you realized to do so would surrender a part of your soul. I'm gratified you didn't. It says a lot to me about who you are."

She nipped at her lower lip. Released it. "Don't hold me up to that kind of an ideal, Pastor Ken. Please. Trust me; I'm nobody's moral barometer."

He shook his head. Restraining the connection to her vanished. He stroked her cheek with a light touch. "Funny. Neither were any of the apostles, the saints, right on back to King David." He shrugged. "We're all flawed, Kiara, so it seems to me you're in good company."

She looked at him, her wide eyes reflecting the patterns and uncertainty of a questing soul.

For now, those words had to be Ken's final say on the subject. He hoped—prayed, in fact—that his words might be enough to spur her onward. He stood and slid from the pew, stepping resolutely into the main aisle. He retreated, seeking the safe haven of his office.

There he could find respite from a woman who played through his heart like a sweet, promising song.

Sitting behind his desk, Ken decided to bury himself in fiscal bureaucracy. It was preliminary budget time, and number crunching would put an end to any kind of romantic revelry. Though he loathed the annual numbers process, he couldn't avoid the matter, so he opened up last year's manila file folder and slid it into place, determined to make progress on the upcoming model.

He pulled open the top drawer of his desk, sifting through clutter in search of a red pen. There, almost hidden beneath a box of paperclips and a square of yellow sticky notes rested a single rectangular admittance ticket, dated just about two years ago.

Woodland Church — Autumn Fest

The sight of it stilled Ken's hand at once. He carefully drew out the ticket, and then stretched back in his chair to study it for a moment. Like a port-key, the small piece of pumpkin colored cardstock sent him reeling backward in time, awash in memories both painful and beautiful. Unable to focus on the here and now, Ken allowed himself to drift.

He sank into the moment completely, reliving that fateful night, and its aftermath, all over again.

In a figurative sense, Barb had twisted his arm to attend the event. She seemed to have recovered well from her two-days-ago chemo treatment and was eager to participate in the festival. It's not that he didn't support and appreciate the event. Instead, Barb's continuing battle with stomach cancer pinned his focus to the exclusion of everything else.

New this time was a parade of costumes. Parishioners, young and old alike, would strut a catwalk that cut through the center of the church activity center.

Committee member Kiara Jordan had coordinated that aspect of the proceedings while Daveny and Elise Edwards championed the music and food/beverage offerings respectively. The event promised to be a huge success, but in truth, Ken had paid attention with only half a heart.

He worried about Barb overdoing it, but had no strength to argue against her wishes. Not after everything she had been through during the past eight months.

"This is just what I need tonight, Ken," she said as they walked into the already crowded hall.

He kissed her cool, pale cheek, smiling down at

her. "I know, so I promise not to be a pest as long as you—"

"Promise to let you know if I start to get tired," she finished, rolling her eyes.

They laughed and she squeezed his arm, her weight transferring to him bit by bit as they neared a table. *Small steps,* he thought. *The treatments mean she'll tire easily, and rebound faster if I let her rest in spells.*

Ken seated her at a table that included the Edwards family so she could visit with friends while he dispensed with some mandatory mingling, and searched for Kiara. During the course of planning meetings, she had worked enough magic to convince Ken to emcee the costume display, so he needed the order of participants and accompanying descriptions.

"Want some pop?" he asked Barb. "There's also some veggies and fruit at the food table, pumpkin bread, too."

"Sure, that'd be great. Thank you."

"Be right back."

He glanced up, at a raised runway, which was the focal point of the room. Tables and chairs surrounded the platform. Behind the runway he saw a curtained off staging area. The curtain, of orange, yellow and deep red, featured an overlay of white netting plastered by vivid colored leaves that had just fallen across the grounds of Woodland. Under Kiara's supervision, the youth group had raked, then created, the display. Further enhancement came in the form of a dozen or so cut outs of pumpkins, cornucopias and shimmery red apples. Cornucopias and a few small pumpkins also served as table highlights.

Ken grinned. Kiara's touch again. She had mobilized the youth group into a decorating frenzy and come up with terrific results. He enjoyed the atmosphere while he stood in line and prepared Barb's soft drink and food plate. He greeted a few parishioners then returned to Barb briefly before leaving to find out more about his emcee duties.

Figuring he'd find Kiara in the staging area, Ken ducked behind the black curtain where fashion show participants had already started to gather. Kiara stood at the center of the crowd, clipboard in hand. She gave him a smile of such warmth and vitality its impact stroked against an unexpected, vibrating spot and brought it to life.

She sported the attire of a woman on safari, right down to the tan colored jacket and matching calf-length shorts. A safari hat rested atop hair plaited into twin braids. Binoculars, of course, dangled from her neck.

"You look great," Ken said when he joined her.

"Our master of ceremonies is here! Hey, Pastor Ken. And don't you look every inch the dashing emcee." She reached up to fuss with the black bow tie at his throat. "Let me guess—you're the groom at the top of a wedding cake?"

He laughed. "Close, but not quite. The tuxedo might lead you to that conclusion, but I'm not a groom—although this is a dual costume with my bride."

"Oh?" She waited on elaboration.

He gave her a sheepish look. "Think about it, Kiara. Barbie and —"

She burst into laughter. "Ken! I love it! I can't wait to see Barb all done up." The jovial moment stilled. "How's she doing?"

Ken couldn't—wouldn't—slide into sadness. Not

right now. "She's fighting hard. She'll love seeing you. She says she's feeling good, but she gets tired fast."

Kiara reached for his hand and gave it a squeeze then offered an ease-restoring grin. "Is she in pink, I hope?"

"Oceans of it, in satin of course, along with a gleaming, way-too-perfect blonde wig." That covers steadily thinning hair, he added in silence. "It's a hoot. She's having fun with it."

"Tell her I'll see her right after the show."

"I will."

From beneath the clip of the board she held, Kiara slipped free a stack of note cards. "Here's your script, in order."

"Thanks."

A young boy with eyes full of moisture and lips quivering stepped up and tugged on Kiara's cropped jacket.

"Miss Kiara, my tail fell off!"

Dejected, this young Mustafa the Lion King offered up a long brown snake of cloth with a fuzzed, fluffy tip. A tear made its way down his plump cheek. Above the boy's head, Kiara gave Ken a quick look before taking her charge by the hand, saying, "No worries. I can fix it. Your costume will be just fine."

"Really?"

"Promise. So, no tears, OK? Remember, you're going to be on stage soon!"

Kiara's excitement turned the tide. Ken watched them walk away while crowds pressed in, increasing the noise level as well as an air of backstage anticipation.

Elise Edwards came charging into the cordoned off space, expelling a huge sigh of relief when she caught sight of him. "Ken. Ken, you need to come with me. Now."

The concerned look on her face prompted him to move fast. She pressed a hand against her chest as they trotted out the doors of the activity center. "Barb had to leave, to go to the ladies room. When she didn't come back right away, I went to check on her. Well…"

Oh no.

Ken pushed into the lavatory without hearing anything else Elise said.

"Barb?" He called with studied calm. He crumbled on the inside when he saw waves of pink satin on the floor of the second stall. She breathed hard, and he could hear her crying. "Barb, honey. Let me in."

"No."

"Sweetheart, please. Let me in."

She didn't reply. A series of tense, silent seconds beat past, but at last the door latch slid slowly free. She didn't rise from her kneeling position on the floor. Ken moved in carefully while she flushed the toilet then wiped a shaky hand across her damp mouth. She began to sob uncontrollably, then choked, "Can you take me home?" She pulled the shimmering wig from her head, leaning her elbows on the bowl. She didn't make eye contact of any kind, she looked shamed, and beyond that, devastated.

"You bet. Come here." Ken lifted her up, alarmed anew by how light she felt, even at a near dead weight.

"I'm sorry, Ken. I'm so sorry."

"Shhh. You have nothing at all to be sorry for."

"I thought I could do this. Honestly I felt fine until I ate."

"I know you did. Don't worry. It's OK now. We'll get you home, you'll get a good night's rest and you'll rebound. Don't worry about it."

He set her gently on her feet, holding her snug to his side. He guided her outside the building, into cool, reviving air.

"Oh, Ken." She paused after whispering the words, breathing deep. "Thank you. This helps a lot. I got so hot, and it hit me so fast."

Despite renewed comfort, Barb's skin remained splotched by the red stains of a blood rush that contrasted violently against the milk-white tone of her skin. He captured her face gently between his hands and looked into eyes that were still too bright.

"Thank you," he said quietly.

"For?"

"For keeping your promise."

He watched her throat work as she swallowed hard. Her eyes filled. "So have you, Ken. You always do. I love you for that, and for so much more."

He touched her cheek, so soft despite her physical battle against illness. "That road works both ways. I love you, too."

He drove the few short blocks home. Barb's head lolled against the seat and she sighed. When they arrived, he nearly called Collin to take his place as emcee, but Barb wouldn't allow it. She needed rest and peace, so he didn't push. Instead, he brewed a mug of green tea for her.

Just looking at her, Ken knew she fought valiantly to keep down the offering, but minutes after settling into place, she calmed. She laid on the couch, beneath a quilt she had made years ago during a church sponsored quilting bee. She looked frail and pale to the point of translucence.

"It's bad this time," she murmured. "I just want to

rest." Tears beaded on her lashes. "I hate that I don't have energy anymore. That I'm not even strong enough to move around. This is horrible."

"I want to stay with you "

"No. Ken, you need to go back to church. They're counting on you."

"So are you. And you're more important than anything else. Period."

She touched his face. When she reached up, he noticed how elongated and too thin her fingers had become. "Will you pray with me, Ken?"

The request melted his soul, poured it free. "Of course."

They joined hands and bowed heads; a fine tremor translated from her hands to his, further depleting his control mechanisms. He closed his eyes, fighting to find the ability to persevere. "Lord Jesus, we pray for the touch of Your healing, for the merciful grace of Your comfort through each and every cell of Barb's body. Give her rest. Bless her with peace and calm in the midst of the storm she faces. Assure her of Your steadfast, faithful love and provision."

"And dear Lord," Barb continued softly, "I pray Your peace and comfort on Ken as he sees to my needs, his own needs, and the needs of Woodland Church. Guide, guard and bless him, dear Lord. He needs Your strength as much as I do."

Ken looked into her eyes as they finished in unison: "In Jesus' name we pray. Amen."

Barb squeezed her lips tight and dashed away the moisture that sparkled at the edges of her eyes. "Now get out of here. Go back to the festival. I can rest now, and it'll do you good to get out for a while. I'll be fine…and you're just a cell call away."

Ken obeyed. Her tired eyes left him no choice.

As ever, especially these days, Woodland and its circle of faith brought him a much-needed sense of normalcy. He still visualized Barb back home, but gradually allowed himself to get into the spirit of the event. In fact, it wasn't long before Kiara peeked out from behind the stage curtain and signaled Ken to start the proceedings.

Amazing to think that only about forty-five minutes had passed since the time they had greeted one another.

Ken gave her a nod. He walked to a podium set up to the right of the catwalk and picked up the microphone. "Welcome to Woodland Autumn Fest, everyone." It was then that he remembered: He had completely lost track of his note cards. He froze for a few seconds—seconds that felt like hours—then did the only thing he could. He began to wing it. "Our charity this year is the Macomb County Shelter, MCS for short. The winter months are coming, and the funds being raised tonight will warm literally hundreds of stranded, displaced homeless people. Thank you for that blessing to our community."

The lights dimmed and the stage became illuminated. He floundered internally but moved on. "So, without further ado, please join me in viewing the very latest in what the best dressed autumn reveler will be wearing this year. It's no trick, just a treat, no matter what your age."

A round of applause gave him time to make eye contact with Kiara. Busy with a hundred details of her own, she had no clue about what had happened to Barb; nor did she realize he had forgotten the note cards. She gave him a thumbs-up and an encouraging nod before sending the first runway participant into the spotlight.

Ken was eternally grateful for the fact that God graced him with a close-knit parish family. He knew, by name, each of the twenty-five participants. As to the costume descriptions, he did the best he could, improvising on the fly. A few times, he caught sight of Kiara in his peripheral vision, watching in puzzlement as he continued. He'd have to explain later.

The last two on parade were Mustafa the Lion, little Jimmy Ginion, and Kiara. Jimmy had re-found his outgoing demeanor now that his tail was back in place; Kiara, meanwhile, vamped like a long-time owner of the runway, watching Mustafa through her binoculars, posing playfully, even cringing when he turned toward her and growled.

Ken continued emceeing. "Last but not least, we have the lovely Kiara Jordan, enjoying a safari-side view of the king of the African plains: Mustafa the Lion."

At the end of the runway, Kiara lifted Jimmy into her arms and paused so they could both acknowledge the applauding crowd. She encouraged Jimmy's enthusiastic waves and they blew kisses toward the audience. The duo left everyone, Ken included, laughing, rejoicing in pure, sweet innocence.

"Kiara, is it smart for safari participants to play with the animals?" Ken couldn't help but tease.

She looked over her shoulder at him and replied handily, "You bet it is, Pastor Ken."

More laughter followed, and applause reached a crescendo while they returned to the staging area. As fast as Ken's energy level had peaked, motivating him to get through the show, it evaporated. He exited the podium as fast as he could, leaning against a check-in table behind the curtain.

Thank you, Lord Jesus. Thank you. I needed you so much, and as always, you faithfully lift me up. Thank you. The prayer sang through his blood stream and soothed a depleted spirit, a tense body.

"Ken?" Very quietly Kiara spoke, stepping up from the buzzing crowd to touch his arm. She smiled, but hesitance shadowed her eyes. "That was quite a show. You were awesome."

He didn't answer. He didn't know what to say.

"What happened?" she asked.

"Lost my note cards."

She didn't take her hand from his arm. The assurance of connecting to someone helped steady him further. Ken breathed deep and could have sworn he came upon her scent—roses, and an undercurrent of vanilla.

"Something happened," she said.

He nodded. "Barb. She got sick a little while after we arrived. I had to get her home, and I just...I...I lost track of everything to be honest. Everything but her."

Kiara looked into his eyes, and her own went full, sparkling in the soft white light coming from overhead. "Which is just as it should be. And P.S.? You were amazing. Tonight shows how connected you are to your church, Ken. You knew every person by name. You brought everyone into the mood and fun, and all the while—all the while you—" Her words softened to nothing more than a whisper as she continued to look at him.

"Don't look at me like that. I just did what I had to do. What she asked me—actually what she forced me to do."

"Ken."

She spoke his name on a breath. She gave him a light, lingering hug then stepped back, brushing tears from her lashes. Meanwhile, he experienced a delayed reaction. He received and accepted her affection, of course, but the essence of her lingered. Surrounded.

Penetrated.

Ken stared at her, not really seeing—only feeling—a spark of life and heat filling his heart.

Kiara continued. "Tell Barb I'm going to stop by. I really did miss seeing her tonight. Would that be OK?"

He found his voice just fast enough to reply, "That would be very OK."

"I'll call first, and make sure she's up to it."

"If she's able, she'll love it."

She nodded. "I'll be there."

After that, it didn't take long for her to get swept into the congratulations and camaraderie of the people who put on the Autumn Fest. Ken, meanwhile, moved quietly, slowly away.

But Kiara didn't make idle offers and let them vanish. The next day, after the promised phone call, she showed up at the front door, arms laden by a white wicker basket overflowing with multi-colored, fall-hued mums.

Ken appreciated the way Kiara focused on Barb, her affection plain as the two women chatted over the steaming mugs of the jasmine tea he prepared. They talked about Kiara's job, happenings at Woodland, they even joked about Barbie attire and platinum blonde wigs. There was no awkwardness Ken could discern, not even at the mention of Autumn Fest. All that flowed between them was easy friendship. The relaxed way Barb related to Kiara assured him that the visit wasn't just welcome, but enjoyed as well.

When Kiara left an hour or so later, he walked her outside, to where her car was parked in the driveway.

"Thanks for coming over," he said. A cool breeze, spiced by the aroma of nearby burning leaves, slid against his face. "The flowers are beautiful. You didn't have to do that."

"I wanted to do that," Kiara answered, sliding a set of keys from her purse and settling the strap on her shoulder. She unlocked the car with a blip of her key-fob then opened the door. When she turned toward him, her lower lip disappeared beneath the press of her teeth. A second later, tears sprang to her eyes and a few of them overflowed. "I don't want her to suffer. She's such a sweetheart."

Her reaction cut Ken to the quick, lancing straight through to the very heart of every fear, every anxiety he possessed. He stuffed his hands into the pockets of his slacks, willing himself not to weaken. Not to crumble like a too-brittle reed.

The effort was wasted.

He pulled his hands free, gathered Kiara into his arms and held on fast. She answered the gesture with equal force and need for support. Ken could summon no resistance to the truth that her touch, the connection they shared, felt beautiful.

Into the moment had ridden a tension-relieving sensation of affirmation and comfort that had played in perfect contradiction to his embroiled spirit.

Leaving memories behind, Ken shook his head and rubbed his eyes. His fingertips came away damp with a few tears that had squeezed free. He sighed, blinking until his vision cleared and the ticket he held came back into focus. His earlier plan to escape Kiara's impact had utterly backfired.

He needed…

One last escape from home—one last respite from the non-stop battle he fought against a loneliness that periodically pervaded and choked his life. He wanted to channel negativity into something positive, a blessing to those in need.

He re-stowed the ticket and straightened, resolved to move forward with a plan that had been percolating in his mind for a few weeks now. He'd conduct a mission trip this coming autumn. Preliminary research had already been completed. The mountains of Pennsylvania called with a need for service, and he wanted Woodland Church to help answer the summons.

Kiara seemed intent on growing her faith walk and relationship with God. If she could help out, so much the better. It might be just the needed way forward—for both of them.

5

To: <u>Kiara.Jordan@Montgomerylandscape1.com</u>;
<u>Daveny.MontgomeryEdwards@Montgomerylands cape1.com</u>
From: <u>Lucerne@WoodlandCC.com</u>
Subject: Lunch?

Do you crave sustenance? Let me know if the two of you can get together for lunch at some point this week. I'll come to Birmingham to make things easier logistically. I'd love to see you, and brainstorm an idea I want to explore...(Are you intrigued yet?)

Ken

Kiara re-read the e-mail from Ken then beelined to Daveny's office. Standing at the threshold, she asked, "Did you see the e-mail from—"

Daveny studied her flat-screen. She chuckled quietly then looked up. "Ken, right?"

"Ah—*yeah.*"

Daveny shrugged, but her eyes sparkled, which further unsettled Kiara's nervous system.

"A warning, my friend," Daveny said. "Take it from someone who knows first hand—Ken Lucerne possesses the gift of sneak-attack."

No kidding. Kiara's heart trip hammered.

"Something's brewing—and he knows just how to draw people in. So beware, my dear."

Fabulous. This was precisely what Kiara needed to hear when just the thought of him made her nerves shiver. "Well it seems, *my dear*, that his e-mail was directed to *both* of us."

Daveny just kept on grinning. "What day works best for you? I'm open this week." Kiara set her jaw, tension and anticipation rolling off her in waves. Meanwhile Daveny waited, calm and unaffected. Further, she arched a brow, prodding. "Well?"

Kiara huffed at her friend's demure posture then muttered, "Thursday."

Daveny nodded. "Thursday it is."

Turning on her heel, Kiara exited the doorway. Daveny's accompanying laughter did nothing at all to sooth Kiara's stirred up senses.

Daveny called sweetly: "Hey, Miss Agitated, shall you reply, or shall I?"

"I'll do it," Kiara cringed because her sharp reply would do nothing but confirm nervousness at spending time with Ken outside the comfort zone of Woodland Church.

"Touchy, touchy," Daveny replied. "By the way? A bistro table in the courtyard at 220 Merrill sounds wonderful…"

A deliberately appealing and relaxing restaurant choice—idyllic in a way—which only worsened Kiara's escalating tensions. With fierce keystrokes, she hit the reply toggle and began to type. She could have left the task of responding to Daveny, but didn't want to. *She* wanted to be the one to connect to him. *She* wanted to see him. But facing that realization scared her to bits at the moment, because in reality the anticipation of seeing Ken outside of church overrode everything else. Pushed. Magnetized. Provoked.

Attracted.

Lord was she was in trouble. Hence, she felt like a trapped grizzly bear.

రావ

Daveny looked crestfallen. "You're leaving? *Again*?"

Ken nodded. "Yes, but only for a week, and this time it involves Woodland. After this mission, I promise, I'm staying put."

"A week in Appalachia." Kiara continued to listen, and watch him. Her words came out as a statement, not a question.

Ken looked at her, and his gaze stayed put for a moment. "With the STAGE group."

Woodland's teen-based service organization. Kiara nodded, still wondering why he needed Daveny's input, or hers. It seemed all systems were go. Why did Ken urge the lunch they now shared? They had claimed a small metal table on the outside patio at 220 Merrill, a favored hot-spot in the heart of a very busy, summer-kissed downtown Birmingham.

Ken continued, his gaze now including Daveny. "Here's where I could use your help. I need volunteers. Daveny, can you help me recruit a few adult chaperones?" While Daveny thought that over, his focus returned to Kiara. "And actually, Kiara, I was hoping you might be able to join the trip."

At that moment, their food arrived—thank

goodness. While the server placed platters, shock swept in. Kiara swallowed hard, staring down at her corned beef on rye.

"Told you I'd remember." Ken said. The soft tone of his voice bore undercurrents of an intimacy that her heart welcomed, even if her head resisted. Heat moved through her body in a rush, speeding upward from her toes straight on through to her dizzying head.

A week. With Ken.

She couldn't quite move past the fact. Meantime, he kept quiet, taking his time about unwrapping cutlery and spreading a linen napkin across his lap. Dressed in crisply pressed tan slacks and a simple blue shirt that he wore un-tucked over a loose white t-shirt, he looked a far cry from the role of preacher. Everything about him spoke of approachability—and male appeal.

Daveny perched her chin on folded hands. "I think I know of a couple people we could approach."

"There'll probably be a dozen or so kids—evenly divided into performance teams—so the way I figure it we need a couple men and a couple women to help oversee everything. Maggie Voorhees, our secretary and youth group director, already signed on."

"So," Daveny said, "you'd be looking for one more woman and two men, right?"

"Yep." He sidled Kiara a look, but that was it.

Shell shocked, Kiara remained a silent observer. She ate, watched and listened, until Daveny slid her cell phone from the pocket of her blazer, checking its face.

"Dang," she muttered. "I've gotta head back to the office."

Kiara snapped to, and her heart leapt into

overdrive. "What? There's nothing on the schedule—"

Daveny grabbed her purse from the spot at her feet and pecked Ken's cheek in passing. "Just came up. Ken, can you take Kiara back to the office?"

"Sure."

"Thanks. Talk to you later. Take your time, though, OK?"

Daveny vanished and Kiara couldn't help being bewildered. A strand of hair rippled across her face. Nervous and shy, she tucked it behind her ear. She tried to focus on lunch, but her appetite no longer existed.

"So," Ken murmured, his focus on his plate. He picked up a section of his turkey club, but didn't bite in right away. He looked uncomfortable as well, and in fairness, Kiara realized she wasn't helping matters by acting like a bewitched teenager.

So she reigned in her poise and pushed disquiet to the side. She gave him a smile. "So."

"I honestly didn't mean for this lunch to turn into an ambush, Kiara." His gaze lifted to hers, and her heart stuttered. That fact she knew without being told.

Conciliatory, she touched his arm. "I'm surprised by the suggestion, but I don't feel ambushed. Please don't worry about that. It does give me a lot to think about, though."

"You came to mind immediately when I planned this trip."

"Really?" She honestly couldn't figure out why that might be, but felt flattered he thought of her.

"Yes, *really*. To me, it's obvious."

Kiara puzzled, and waited on elaboration. Realizing that, Ken's smile dawned as warm as spring sunlight.

"Kiara, stop being the deer that's caught in the headlights. You're a natural to work with. You'll be more than able to guide and engage a group of teenagers. Remember how well you handled preps for Autumn Fest?"

Her heart went light at his praise; at the same time, a lance of painful memory pierced her spirit. *Barb.* "That was years ago, and…and, that was *easy.*"

He gave her a pointed look. "Do you think so?"

To fill time, Kiara broke their visual connection and munched on a chip. She hoped to disguise her turmoil and deflect the power of his appeal. Being attracted to him, considering the prospect of intense, out-of-church interaction, left her with a mid-section full of tickling, dancing butterfly wings.

The idea tempted, but at the same time, the thought of participating in a Christian service mission removed her far—make that *very* far—from her comfort zone. Still, she melted into a form of mental surrender. Mission work would fill an empty spot in her spirit, a need and a call to do something *more.* Most likely, Ken sensed that fact as well—he was as perceptive as he was caring. Dogging Kiara's heels of late nipped the feeling that her life lacked merit beyond that of being arm candy for sexy, successful men. A chic fashionista. Didn't she feel increasing unease about being seen as nothing more than a honey-blonde who could attract attention as easily as nectar attracted bees?

The life she embraced up to now left her empty, and wanting. Had for years. Ever since meeting Ken— ever since joining Woodland Church—she had discovered a world outside her heretofore narrow focus.

As though reading her mind, he leaned forward, closing their slight physical distance. He was intent and *enthused*. That snared her heart like nothing else could, and filled Kiara with longing. In the end, she wanted to live up to the promise Ken saw inside her.

"I've participated in a few missions recently. I know what I'm doing. You're a special lady. I'd love for you to participate, and get a sense of what these trips accomplish. The joy and hope and freedom a little help from people like us can give to these people is amazing. One week away from everything you know, and all that's familiar, is going to bring you to a place in your life and your walk with God that nothing else can match." His eyes fixed on Kiara, drawing her in—a most seductive impetus. "It'll be a gift, Kiara. In so many ways..."

His full lips, the tumbled wavy brown hair that danced in a gentle breeze, left her transfixed. Wistful—*in so many ways.*

"Do me a favor?" He asked.

She nodded numbly.

"Will you *consider* it? I understand it's a lot to ask. I know being a part of this trip would mean sacrificing a week of vacation time from your job, but..."

His voice trailed off. The impact of his gaze did not. Like she could refuse satiny eyes of chocolate brown—

She caught her breath. "Of course I'll think about it. The offer has taken me by surprise, that's all."

They concluded their lunch companionably, and she had to admit that once she moved past the initial bout of giddiness Ken's presence stirred, the surprise generated by his mission suggestion, she found it easy to settle into a comfortable rhythm. They caught up with one another and enjoyed lunching outdoors on a gorgeous afternoon.

Much as she hated for the interlude to end, soon enough work schedules called and Ken accompanied her back to the office.

There, Daveny waited.

And there certainly didn't seem to be a work-related fire going on that Kiara could detect.

She deposited her purse in a desk drawer then paid her partner and best friend a visit in her office. True to sassy form, Daveny wasted no time on preamble. "When do you leave for Pennsylvania?"

"As soon as I find out about the big corporate emergency you're taking care of," Kiara shot back.

Daveny just blinked prettily. "Emergency? What emergency?"

Kiara's jaw dropped. "Daveny Montgomery Edwards. Are you attempting a set up?"

"Everyone needs a hobby."

Kiara sank into the chair before Daveny's desk, expelling a hard, tense breath. "Do you realize this would mean *six* hours. In a *van*." *In close, intimate proximity*, she neglected to add. "What in the world am I going to talk about with him? What'll we say?"

"First off, let me enlighten you. I've helped Collin out in his high school English classes from time to time, doing organizational things and the like. I've gotten to know teenagers. Therefore, I can assure you, conversation will be the least of your worries. This trip to the Appalachians is going to be anything but *quiet*. Furthermore, I think you realize that fact without being told. Since that's the case, I have to ask, Kiara, what's scaring you?" Daveny's eyes narrowed. "Because quite frankly, I'm *stunned*. When have you ever—I repeat—

ever been timid about making conversation with a man?"

Kiara's cheeks stung and prickled, the first alert of a dawning blush. "Dav, come on. You know what I mean. I'll be with Pastor Ken."

"Oh. I see. And as opposed to being a man, Ken's a *zombie,* is that the issue?"

"Pastor Ken," Kiara corrected. A touch of something sensuous and enticing skirted her nerve endings.

"Ken." Daveny answered right back. "And he's just a man."

"Thanks for illuminating, but that's not my point. I'm just not sure what we're going to have to say to each other during the course of this proposed mission. We're so *different."*

"Nice try, but I'm not buying. Kiara, you're afraid of him."

"Am not!"

"I don't mean afraid like Jack-the-Ripper afraid, I mean afraid in a completely different way, and I think you know exactly what I'm talking about." Kiara moved hastily to cut her off, but Daveny quelled a reply by simply lifting her hands. "Proof? Allow me to take you back a few years. You and I were neck deep in a church renovation, remember?'

Kiara remained still, but inwardly fought against the sensation of being cornered by her own heart.

"You sat in that very chair, telling me how much you enjoyed Ken's company, how much you liked him and wished the quote-unquote *good ones* like him weren't already taken."

Kiara squirmed but Daveny kept going. "You longed for a connection to him, but he was married.

Off limits." Shaking her head vigorously, staring into Kiara's eyes, Daveny concluded firmly. "Well he's not off limits anymore."

Like a temptation, that idea dangled before Kiara's thirsty, wanting heart.

And Daveny went on. "He's a man of meaning, a man of depth and substance. He's exactly the kind of man you know you want and need, yet for some reason his attainability has you running for cover." Daveny relented, leaning back once again. "I won't put you on the spot and ask you for reasons why; your face alone tells me I've hit the mark. What I'm saying, sweetie, is that you need to look at that fact more closely. You need to ask yourself why that's the case. Are you afraid of a genuine commitment from a genuine man? Before you answer, I have to I warn you, he'll want it all. He's not after a trophy girl, or instant gratification, but is instead searching for a woman who possesses equal parts substance and beauty. Someone just like you."

"Daveny, he's clergy! He's a man of God. I'm…I'm…Cosmo's with my girlfriends after work. I've had a few casual relationships based on sex appeal and charisma…and…and…" At last, Kiara came out with what she considered the deepest problem. "Dav, the point is, I'd be no good for him. I could never make him happy. Not over the long term. You talk about his substance, and that's exactly what draws me to him. I'll admit that freely. But I'm sorely lacking in the things he needs most."

"Bull!"

"It's true. I'm these looks, and this body, and I've let myself be taken in by flash too many times to ever believe a man like *Ken* could find me suitable. Come on. Seriously. Me? The paramour of a preacher?"

Undeterred Daveny just shrugged. "Why not, Kiara? Why not?"

And one thing was for certain. Mona Lisa's enigmatic turn of lips had nothing on the smile currently displayed on the face of Kiara's best friend.

ॐॐ

Nervousness got the better of her. Kiara could own that fact. She could deal with it. She closed and locked the door of her apartment then trotted to her car. Once there she realized she had forgotten her notebook. Checking her watch, she took in how close she cut her arrival time. She didn't want to be late to the mission trip orientation meeting, but ran back to retrieve the notebook, anyway.

The four-mile drive to Woodland turned into an exercise in finding every red light and slow-moving vehicle in the city of St. Clair Shores, which meant there was too much time to think about Ken, and the idea of actually participating.

With *him*.

The thought followed her to the church parking lot. Kiara left her car and then remembered the notebook still rode shotgun. What was the message here? There had to be a message.

Maybe: *Don't even try.* Or perhaps: *Don't worry about notes, be more concerned with what's written on your heart.*

She mentally admitted her betting money went on the latter option. Still, after an exasperated sigh, she retrieved the wire-bound source of her aggravation and marched through the entrance of Woodland.

Resolute—defiant in fact—Kiara walked the long, narrow corridor to the left of the narthex. Along the way, she passed a number of darkened classrooms and conference rooms. She found her way to the brightly lit gathering spot indicated on Ken's e-mail: Conference Room 1D.

And the most amazing thing happened.

Peace flooded her, unstoppable because it took her by such surprise. Calming peace and a soothing sense of assurance wrapped around her like a tender hug. She absorbed Woodland's familiar flower and must scent, the stillness and quiet of the building. The moment did what nothing else could right now— telegraphed God's presence.

In that instant, she stopped fighting herself.

After signing in, she looked around, cataloguing attendees. A dozen or so teens buzzed amongst themselves, a tight knit group huddled at the long table up front. Talk about multi-tasking—most of them sent text messages, laughed, talked, carried on phone conversations and picked at one another simultaneously. Kiara smiled at the exuberant behavior.

Pastor Ken stood at the head of the teen table, somehow able to focus despite the relentless clamor. The sight of him stalled her at the welcome desk. She noticed the way he gnawed on the end of a pen, reading a paper he held.

"Kiara, are you set?"

"What?" She turned to look at Margaret Voorhees, Woodland's church secretary, who also coordinated youth group activities and had helped implement the upcoming mission trip. Since attendance was completed, Margaret watched her curiously. "Oh.

Yeah. I'm fine, thanks."

Kiara moved away, taking note of a white vinyl banner that covered the wall to her right. Painted a variety of bright colors, the sign read: WELCOME TO THE STAGE!

She stepped up to the table where Ken stood.

"Hi," she greeted tentatively. And she couldn't help wondering where the fluttery, bashful vibe of hers was coming from these days. The look in Ken's eyes warmed her senses, set assurance and welcome sailing through her body.

"Hey! I'm glad you're here. Take the seat by me."

"OK." Kiara returned his smile, but looked away shyly, reacting instantly to his warm kindness. She deposited her notebook and trip materials on the table then checked out the sign a bit more closely, reading its subtext aloud: "Super Teen Angels Go Evangelize."

Ken glanced over his shoulder and looked at the sign as well. He nodded. "STAGE. It's our name, and our mantra. Plus, they're at such a formative age. When necessary, the STAGE name makes it easier for them to talk about meetings and group events without risking stigma."

That kind of pressure Kiara understood. "I can imagine."

"Especially for teenagers dealing with their peers, and type-casting, it's important to live their Christian faith, not lose confidence as they're teased about church related meetings and being part of a youth ministry."

"Like that old saying: Live the Gospel—use words only if necessary."

"Exactly." He filled two Styrofoam cups with ice water and handed her one. She accepted his thoughtful gesture with a smile; her fingertips trailed against his, drawing their eyes into a brief, stirring connection before he walked away.

Ken crossed the room, calling for everyone's attention and quiet. Kiara took her seat as he clicked off the overhead lights. A laptop was set up at his spot on the table. When Ken returned, he began the proceedings. "Meet the Kidwell family."

Click by click, he took the potential attendees through a computerized slideshow presenting each needy family member. First came the young mother, Casey; then Phillip, the oldest boy and freshly minted teenager who smiled shyly for the camera. Next came six-year-old twins, Amber and Alyssa, who both possessed such sparkle and spunk their images leapt from the display screen.

In conclusion, however, he returned to the image of Casey Kidwell. Long brown hair was tied into a simple ponytail. Her fair features were plain, but clear and clean. Jeans and a t-shirt were nondescript, but her eyes were large and wide, retaining an innocence that left Kiara moved.

Pastor Ken continued. "Casey struggles to make ends meet. Her sense of hope? It gets trampled on every day because, as her application states, she feels all alone in the fight to keep her family safe and well provided for."

Silence filled the room as he continued. "This trip is about service, and it's about helping a struggling family find hope, but as many of you know, lately I've spent a lot of time lending assistance to missions very similar to the one I propose to you right now. So let me assure you of something." He paused strategically and performed a slow, deliberate survey of the posture, faces and eyes of the dozen or so teens and the sprinkling of adults who gathered. "Beyond heeding God's call to uplift those who need it the most, this trip will transform you. It's as much about evolution, and advancing your own spiritual walk, as it is about applying fresh layers of paint, cleaning, or planting trees. You'll be the face of Christ to our needy brothers and sisters, but don't expect to walk away from the experience without being changed."

A murmur of acceptance and agreement circuited the room.

"So…details about the mission. If you open your folders, you'll find an itinerary that outlines the details and goals of the program. We're headed to Zion Grove, in the Appalachian Mountains."

Kiara followed along, reviewing statistics and overall program information.

Ken went on. "A community of nine families is living below poverty levels and has been identified by the Christian Youth Outreach Program. What that means is we won't be alone in this. Nine other church-based teams are headed to Pennsylvania to help refurbish homes and reestablish these individuals into lives restored by hard work and a helping hand."

"Where are we going to be staying, Pastor Ken?"

Kiara looked down the table, at the bright-eyed, blonde-haired teen who asked the question. Amy, her nametag read. Ken lifted a color brochure from inside his folder and held it up. "If you pull out this flyer about Red Ridge Lake, I think your questions will be answered. The program we're participating in will take over a small campground. The Woodland team will be responsible for our own meals, cooking and cleanup, but we'll share ministry with the other attendees. We'll be in cabins, four volunteers and one chaperone to each. My hope is to take a dozen members of STAGE and recruit four adult volunteers."

"I don't know anything about, like, home repairs and stuff. What about that?"

Kiara smiled at the second teen who spoke up, a lanky, sandy-haired boy seated next to Amy. Tyler was his name. Kiara readily understood his eager, if somewhat intimidated demeanor.

"Contracted professionals who donate their time will oversee the heavy lifting—stuff like drywall, carpeting and cabinetry. You'll be helping, not supervising, so no worries. You'll get training and tools without a problem."

Questions continued and more details were ironed out while the meeting progressed.

Slowly, Kiara was drawn into the idea of being a part of it all. A tremor from within brought her to the realization that walking away from this opportunity wouldn't be an option. The faces of the Kidwell family, freeze-framed on the wall to her left, pulled at a need in her heart to help. To be present.

At the end of the meeting she hung back, not eager to leave Ken's company. Here she felt assured. Here she felt affirmed and cared for.

The room emptied, and she helped disconnect and store computer parts, then stack up extra information packets while Ken said goodnight to Maggie Voorhees.

When he turned back and saw the results of Kiara's work, he looked pleasantly surprised. "Wow. Thanks."

"No problem."

"Seriously, I appreciate it."

He tossed cups and napkins into the trash. "So

what did you think?" He lingered as well, taking his time about packing supplies into his carryall.

"Well, I think this is a departure for me. It's service, and of course I like that, but it's not like anything I've ever done before."

"Service is what you've provided to Woodland ever since you joined us, Kiara. This trip isn't much different from that."

He nodded toward the chairs they had occupied during the meeting and Kiara made herself comfortable at the table. "But the service you're talking about was provided on a much smaller scale, Pastor Ken." At last she came out with the truth—her biggest fear. "It's intimidating. Am I really up to this? Am I qualified? I'm just not sure, and I don't want to mess things up." She watched for any telltale reactions, but his presence soothed, a gentle oasis in the desert of her unease. "Really. Think about it. Who do I think I am, being a mission participant for heaven's sake?"

"For heaven's sake indeed," Ken quipped in turn.

He looked down at his folded hands. They rested close to Kiara's, and she tingled with a need to touch him. She didn't. Again and again she kept thinking, Pastor. Modernista. Conservative. Contempo. Oil. Water.

Disquiet simmered though her bloodstream, but combating that onslaught rushed a longing that poured through her thick and warm, a quest for...for *something*. Something more than the world, the time and place she currently inhabited. To share an experience like this with Ken? Her mind raced even faster.

"You're stepping off a ledge, Kiara. I understand that. Just remember; the hardest part is letting go."

Their gazes aligned and Ken slid her notebook out of the way. Leaning close he tucked his hand over hers on the tabletop. Her mouth went dry, and she fought hard to focus. "Look at this as an opportunity, I've pushed you. Maybe I shouldn't have. The thing is, though, ever since I've met you, it seems you've been moving into something larger than yourself. You attend church here regularly, but beyond being a *worshiper*, you've *contributed*. I'd love to see that continue. It's been beautiful to watch."

In a perfectly sequenced activation process, his words slid into her then through her. She caught her breath, looking into eyes of deep, velvety brown, falling headfirst. She allowed herself to enjoy the luxury of their soft tenderness.

"This isn't just about opportunity. It's about *ability*. Abilities you possess, Kiara. You're a natural motivator, and the kids love you." He lifted his hand from hers and ticked off a couple more attributes on his fingers. "You magnetize, and you galvanize. You have more energy, spirit and enthusiasm than most people I know. Plus, you draw people in. You can lead."

Silence held sway. She couldn't help thinking about the fact that every word he spoke worked through the spots in her psyche that most craved affirmation and the knowledge that her life, her actions, could have meaning. And, to be validated by a man of such...

Substance and honor.

Daveny's words came back to haunt Kiara—circling around to the one who sat before her, calm and confident, charismatic in his own powerful right. But he was a *pastor*—a chief custodian of God's mission on earth. Her more secular, world-driven life contradicted that pathway. What could ever come to be between the two of them?

It would never work.

Still, her heart swelled, lessening the impact of that thought. Her skin warmed.

Nonplussed by her silence, he continued. "Your instinct may be to step back, and then away, thinking this may be more than you want to take on. I'd only ask you set those feelings aside and take a hard look at the good you'll do. The benefit you'll provide to this family. Think it over. Give it some serious prayer time. If your answer is no after that, then please know I understand. I just don't want you to reject it out of hand because it's something so new, and different for you—or worse yet because you're afraid of a faith jump. You've come so far, so quickly. You're on an important mission, Kiara, whether you join us in Pennsylvania or not. OK?"

She diverted her attention and reclaimed the information folder, fiddling with its edges while silence played out. His words, his spirit loosened her control grips, and left her wanting to fly. "I'm serious about this, Pastor Ken, and I do promise to think everything over very carefully. I just…is it wrong of me to want a little time? A few days maybe? I know my yes should be automatic."

As automatic as my 'No' should have been to Andrew and his offering of a sensual odyssey to Europe. Being a mixed-up mess, spiritually speaking, seemed par for the course these days.

Ken didn't seem to mind. He just nodded and said, "Take what time you need, Kiara. I'll be here."

6

"OK, gang," Ken called. "Let's gather up and finish check-in. We need to hit the road."

Duffle bags decorated the asphalt in front of two vans parked before the entrance of Woodland. He surveyed the milling group of slouching, subdued teenagers dressed in blue jeans, t-shirts and hoodies. There were sixteen in all—yawning and murmuring to one another as dawn crept across the sky. Pale blue turned to mauve, turned to orange then pink behind clouds skirting inland over the horizon of Lake Saint Clair. He leaned against the front of the church's old, reliable standby—an F-250 van—consulting a clipboard of attendees. Dressed in jeans as well, sporting a sweatshirt from his alma mater of Wayne State University, he began to account for staff and teen volunteers.

Daveny drove up, and his focus zipped far from registrations and attendance; Kiara rode shotgun. The car rounded into the lot where Daveny parked then popped the trunk. Kiara climbed out and for a moment, he stood transfixed. Forcing himself forward, Ken moved toward the two women. Kiara tucked a pair of oversized black sunglasses on top of her head. Her eyes roved the assemblage. She nibbled her lower lip, a tiny furrow appearing above her brows while she looked around.

Kiara Jordan, the quintessence of feminine confidence, gave every indication of being tentative. *Beguilingly* tentative, he amended with a push to his heart that enlivened his spirit.

A week—in service with Kiara. The push exploded into a heady rush of anticipation, and joy.

"Hey." He stepped forward, taking the suitcase from Kiara's hand to lighten her load. Her grip was tight, though, and his action took her by surprise judging by the way her gaze lifted to his. She cleared her throat softly and relaxed a bit, surrendering the luggage.

Daveny gave Ken a knowing glance; she hugged Kiara and delivered a wax-coated bakery sack into Kiara's custody. "Don't forget this. Have fun, girlie."

Kiara nodded, continuing to study her surroundings. Ken longed to assure, to draw her in. He understood her reaction. His first few mission trips had featured just such nervousness. Stepping into the unknown never came easy, so all he could do for now was lead her away from Daveny's safe zone.

Daveny, meanwhile, returned to her car and drove away. Distraction might do the trick, Ken figured. So he started to fill in details to help set Kiara's mind at ease. "We've got a two van convoy." A vague gesture indicated both vehicles. "Maggie and her husband are in charge of the second vehicle. I figure you and I will take charge of this one." He patted the engine hood of the Woodland van, and she looked it over.

"Just tell me what I need to do." The words came out heavy, and uncharacteristically shy.

He set her suitcase aside to take her hands, stilling her progress toward check in. "First?" He waited 'til she made eye contact. "What I need you to do is rest easy. OK?"

A pause fell between them. She looked down, seeming embarrassed. Ken quirked a finger beneath her chin and drew her gaze to his once more. "Let go of everything else and embrace the opportunity." He couldn't fight the tremors being near her stirred, nor the hot, dissolving sensation that moved through his body when he took a tumble into her clear, green eyes. "I'm not used to you being unsettled. Relax, Kiara." An intent interlude passed before he concluded, "Here's the itinerary." He handed her a folder, which she accepted with a nod. Her attention reverted to the van. Ken embraced the opening. "Don't worry about her. She's still got plenty of life left where it counts."

Kiara smiled. *Really* smiled. "I'm not worried. I trust the mechanic."

Her glance swept over him in a visual caress, gliding down the front of his sweatshirt, causing an electric circuit to zing to completion. He now realized a smudge of oil residue dotted the bottom edge of the shirt from when he had double-checked engine and fluid levels a few minutes ago.

His tone went huskier than usual. "We don't have the money for a new vehicle, so I work on it, and keep it in shape. Hones my mechanical skills and gives me a sense of accomplishment. So far, so good."

Kiara fumbled a bit with the folded edges of the baker's bag she held. Meanwhile, he retrieved her suitcase and stowed it in the back.

"So," she said, "are you hungry?"

"Always." Ken accepted the bag she offered and opened it wide. Swirls of warmth, and the aroma of cinnamon and apple, wafted upward on a tempting cloud of steam. He peeked inside, marveling. "Fresh apple fritters? Kiara, you're amazing."

She laughed. "Yeah. Shopping at a store for baked goods puts me right up there with the saints."

"In my eyes it does."

Ken leaned down and slid his lips against her cheek, ending the connection in a kiss that lingered too long—yet not long enough. He pulled back and her widened eyes struck a chord in his soul. He stroked the skin he had just kissed with a trailing fingertip then tore off a piece of fritter and ate. The confection melted on his tongue, melting into tasty sweetness.

Kiara followed his lead.

"There's a thermos of Italian roast between the front seats. Coffee is the only way I knew I'd survive," he told her.

"That goes for me, too. Thanks for thinking of it."

He continued to eat while she spoke.

"I wish…"

She came up short. Curious, Ken prodded. "What do you wish?"

"I wish…I wish I didn't feel so much like a fish out of water."

He returned the bag to Kiara so she could eat the second fritter. When she tried to take the bag from his grip, Ken held fast until he won her full focus. "If it helps, remember you're surrounded by friends, and you're doing something miraculous. Further? The kids will adore you."

Deflecting her gaze, Kiara murmured, "How do you *do* that?"

"Do what?"

"I swear, it's a gift, the way you can look into a person and see exactly what they're feeling."

Her words struck home, glided against him like a

provocative ripple of silk. Pleasure sizzled through his body. "It's a job hazard—part of what I do." Beauty and grace, sweetness—all of the most attractive elements of her personality combined to leave him bold, and intrigued enough to say, "Besides, Kiara, everything you are is right there—in your eyes, and on your face. Open book. It's not hard to see what you're feeling. I like that about you." Ken took a meaningful pause. "Here's what else I do."

Ken took her free hand in his. With a nod and a gentle tug, he walked her toward a secluded spot on the other side of the van. Wearing a puzzled expression, Kiara glanced around for a moment—at the quiet roadway, at the fragrant, shimmering grass kissed by morning dew, and the waking shoreline of Lake Saint Clair.

It was perfect.

Ken kept hold of her hand, and said in a whisper, "Pray with me? Privately? Before we do so with the others?"

Her hold on his hand weakened, but not in refusal. Her eyes, wide and wistful, touched on his; she seemed eager to share the moment, and Ken realized the weakness wasn't weakness at all. It was a melting. A surrender to something powerful, intimate, and graced. In silence, she nodded.

He bowed his head, murmuring into the quiet air, "Lord, you've granted us an opportunity to serve You, to lend assistance to the most needy of our brothers and sisters. Keep us strong. Keep us centered in your will, your plans and provision. Lord, in a special way, please bless Kiara as she reaches out in mission for the first time. Show her Your calm and love. Keep us all safe. In Jesus' name we pray."

"Amen," came the unison conclusion. Birds began chirping, starting to arise from towering tree branches that rustled in the building breeze. Ken released her hand, but glided a touch upward, against her arm. "So about that feeling of intimidation? It's God's now. Leave it right here in the parking lot. You're not going to regret this, I promise. And you're most certainly not alone."

He continued to look into her eyes, lingering over a final peaceful moment. Her answering nod and the squeeze of her hand against his arm reassured.

"Ken?" Maggie Voorhees stepped up, her brows knit as she studied them. It occurred to Ken that he stood very close to Kiara, his arm nearly around her, their eyes connected, their posture eloquent in its intimacy. "Everyone's here and supplies are loaded. We're ready for the group send-off and prayer."

"Exactly what I was thinking," Ken replied. Reluctant to end the moment, he knew he had to turn away. Praying with Kiara had been spontaneous and stirring, but the team needed to get going. Besides, he'd have hours of travel time with her, and for now, he wanted to stymie the inquisitive, darkened expression on Maggie's face.

❧

The mission squad barely crossed the state line of Ohio before debate broke out over potential movies to watch.

"Little Women? No *way*! That movie is so *lame*!" Charlie, one of the teen volunteers spoke up first—and with emphasis.

"You get to pick the next movie," said Amy, the

spokeswoman for the women. "We're going to be here for a while, guys. Compromise, right? And PS? Deal with it. It's a good movie."

"C'mon, it'll be fine," said Tyler quietly. Tyler was one of the shyer members of the posse.

"Whatever," groused Alex, another of the Woodland teens.

"Groan!" said David. "Never have I been so grateful for an iPod."

Kiara looked over her shoulder to monitor the crew. Ken glanced into the rearview mirror just in time to see David tune out, white ear buds stuffed into place. The youth fingered his iPod, then closed his eyes and settled in for a doze. The other guys in the group pretty much followed suit.

Amy, Carlie, Liz and Jen—the ladies of the van— shared a grin at their victory. Amy pushed the DVD into a portable player. The foursome shifted seats until they were tucked together to watch. When the movie began to play, Ken shared a wry look with Kiara, and a grin.

Tyler remained quiet thereafter, seeming immune to the teen-style negotiation process. Instead of an iPod connection, he opted to page through a guitar magazine. Ken kept tabs on him and Amy because there seemed to be undercurrents flowing between the two. Well, on Tyler's part anyway. Ken noticed the way Tyler sat to the side and periodically watched the bubbly, blonde.

That in mind, Ken looked sidelong at the gorgeous woman who rode next to him and found he could completely relate to the longing he detected in Tyler's eyes.

They rumbled along, and the movie played.

Dialogue drifted through the vehicle. On screen, Meg had just returned to her loving, though humble home following a society coming out party. Meg conversed with Marmee about its aftermath:

"I liked to be praised and admired," Meg said. *"I couldn't help but like it."*

"Of course not," Marmee answered. *"I only care what you think of yourself. If you feel your value lies in being merely decorative I fear that someday you might find yourself thinking that's all you really are. Time erodes all such beauty. What it cannot diminish are the wonderful workings of your mind. Your humor, your kindness, your moral courage, those are the things I so admire in you."*

Kiara sat quietly and listened, but Ken noticed a turnabout in her mood. Her effervescence dimmed over the next long stretch of highway. Intending to call her out, he reached behind the seat and secured a pair of cups. Next, he lifted the thermos of coffee. "Interested?"

She nodded and smiled. But the quick gesture struck him as false. "Thanks. Here, let me pour."

"You got quiet all of a sudden."

"Yeah. I suppose I did."

The soft-spoken words did nothing to remedy his concern. Neither did the manner in which she turned her head after settling his cup into the holder between them. Looking out the window, she sipped her coffee.

Rather than press, he watched her, indulging a desire to soak her in. The details of her captivated him. A windbreaker, worn to ward off the morning chill, now resided over the back of her seat. She paired a sleeveless, sunshine yellow blouse with tan Capri's. A yellow ribbon wound through the French braid of her hair, securing its end and trailing loose a few inches beyond.

The accessory intrigued him. Considering what it would feel like to slide that piece of satin ribbon free came at him hard, prompting him to look elsewhere in a denial both physical and emotional.

The trip progressed in a mix of movie dialogue, chatter, and an underlying buzz of music from MP3 devices played at decibels only the young could tolerate. Soon the massive state of Pennsylvania welcomed the caravan. The road turned hilly, punctuated by deep, picturesque valleys. Lush green land was dotted by homes and white, clapboard churches became focal points with steeples that soared skyward. Around the valleys rose a rim of mountains skirted by the tree-lined highway.

That's when Ken proposed a 'getting to know you' exercise.

"Kiara," he began, "make a list of five items you see somewhere in the vehicle. It can be anything, but it has to be something here with us."

Everyone started to look around and chatter. Kiara asked, "Can I get some help from the team?"

"Absolutely."

For the next few minutes, the kids called out things they saw and Kiara drafted a list.

"Crayons, from the gift basket we made for the family."

"Bottled water."

"A hoodie!"

"Pop!"

"There's a box of rubber bands back here."

Ken glanced back for a second. "I wondered where those ended up. Thought I had left them at the store."

Seeming puzzled, Kiara kept sidling him glances;

Ken remained silent.

"We're all set," Kiara said. "Now what?"

"Write one of our names by each item, starting with mine and yours."

She scribbled, looking more confused than ever. He grinned—and relented. "Let me show you how the game is played. Kiara, what's the item by your name?"

"Pop."

Ken nodded, and thought about pop for a minute. "How is Kiara like pop?"

Everyone burst out laughing. "Seriously?" One of the mission members asked. "We're comparing ourselves to the things on the list?"

"No. Starting with me, the person sitting next to you is." He began again. "Kiara is like pop because she's bubbly. Just like pop, when you take her in, her spirit sparkles through you."

She turned to listen, leaning her back against the door. Ken's words caused her to stare, her lips slightly parted. Luminous eyes drew him in, just like when they had prayed. That particular recollection causing a spark—like sweet, cool pop—and Ken knew he needed to move things along, fast, before the kids caught on.

"I'm next, right?" Ken asked.

Kiara blinked. "Ah...yeah."

"What item did you assign to me?"

She toyed with the edges of the paper she held, the list on her lap now of paramount importance. "Bottled water."

"OK. How am I like bottled water?"

She blew out a breath, shrugged shyly, and fidgeted with the pen she held. "Pastor Ken is like bottled water because he's...he's clear. And pure. He has a kindness that's thirst-quenching and a heart that gives to others and refreshes. Just like water."

She never glanced his way. She didn't need to. The words spoke strong, and the heat index shot upward. He realized for certain this woman was unaccustomed to being out of her comfort zone with a man.

She recovered fast though, turning to Tyler. "You're next, and you're talking about Amy. Amy's name is by crayons."

Chortles filled the air, prompting Kiara to retort, "Yuck it up for now, hot-shots, but you're all going to have a turn."

He marveled anew at her ease with the teens and kept tabs via the rearview mirror, noting the way Tyler looked at Amy with surprising steadiness. Amy, meanwhile, watched him right back and waited, sliding a strand of hair behind her ear.

Following a brief pause, he answered the question. "Amy is like a box of crayons because she's bright and she has lots of different parts to her personality—like crayon colors. You can use them to crate artwork, and things that are beautiful. When you open a box of crayons, it's kind of like seeing a rainbow."

That shut up the raucous comments, and Amy looked a little breathless. Kiara, fortunately, kept matters going. "OK, Amy, you're up. How is Tyler like...a rubber band?"

Amy groaned and Tyler rolled his eyes, seeming to expect the worst.

"Well," she began in a tentative voice, "I think Tyler is kinda like a rubber band 'cause rubber bands are flexible. They expand when they need to, and they're resilient. They're dependable in that they always go back to what they were once you're done." Then she really warmed up, looking him straight in the eye. "Plus, when you pluck a rubber band after you've pulled it tight, it makes *music*."

Amy's final comment caused Tyler to look at her in sharp surprise. Amy just arched a brow, an all-knowing look in her eyes.

"Carlie," Kiara said, helping move past Amy and Tyler's interlude. "You're up next..."

❧❦

A narrow gravel road led uphill to a series of small, mom-and-pop owned stores along with a dozen or so homes. This wasn't a neatly organized setting, however. The area was time worn and suffered from a state of near-terminal neglect. The neglect, Ken knew from research, didn't stem from uncaring inhabitants, but rather a lack of funds, time and ability. So, mission teams from across the country converged on this tiny, poverty-stricken village to lend assistance. A few vans similar to those from Woodland were parked in the street and clusters of people walked about exploring.

Ken pulled the van to a stop in front of the dilapidated structure owned by Casey Kidwell. For a time, silence reigned within the vehicle. Everyone looked outside, surveying the scene. Clapboard siding was separated in spots to show gaping holes. The roof sagged, and a corner of it looked to be missing completely. Overgrown shrubs and plant life masked a porch that also sagged and featured rotted openings in spots—the product of neglect.

Woodland's arrival prompted the Kidwell family to emerge from inside. Volunteers exited the van and Amy lifted the gift basked into her arms. Amy hesitated at the family's enthusiastic onrush. "Gee, it's like an episode of that home makeover show or something," she said.

True enough. The entire team soon found itself engulfed by hugs, and Casey Kidwell's grateful tears punctuated her appreciation. Amy handed the gift basket to Casey, who let the two youngest kids dive into the contents. The twin girls tugged Amy right down on the front yard grass and pulled her in to explore; the rest of the team joined in on a celebration that looked more like Christmas than the offering of a simple gift basket.

Ken kept an eye on the proceedings and then followed Casey into the house, with Kiara at his side. Soon he discovered just how big a task lay ahead.

Casey, a shy and diminutive woman, ushered them across the threshold, but her demeanor struck him as weighted, and oppressed. "I just want you to know; I'm embarrassed to show you how we've been living. I'm so ashamed, but there hasn't been any other way, and all we wanted to do was stay in our home—such as it is."

Ken rested an arm around her shoulder. "Please don't be uncomfortable. We understand where you're coming from; that's why we want to help."

She looked at him in silence then nodded, leading the way through the house. The tour didn't take long, considering its small size and shotgun style composition. Brief discussions ensued amongst the team members who filtered in. Ken listened, but paid particular attention to the way Kiara absorbed the scene. She trailed fingertips against a patchwork quilt drawn between the kitchen and living room as a makeshift door. She looked out windows covered by cloudy, scarred sheets of plastic designed to add protection from the outside elements. Living room furniture, spare to say the least, had passed the "timeworn" mark long ago. A stale, musty smell permeated the house.

Kiara's eyes went somber, her demeanor subdued.

Two tiny bedrooms skirted a narrow hallway of barren, distressed wood. The bathroom clung to usefulness by virtue of nothing more than heavy globs of caulk and duct tape. Chips and stains dotted the tub, sink and walls.

When they returned outside, Ken made sure to pass by Kiara. Shell shocked, eyes wide, she scanned the scene, her lips down turned. He gave her hand a discreet, understanding squeeze.

In reply to the gesture she firmed her chin and stated quietly, "I can't wait to get started."

The comment warmed his blood. Supermodel looks and her chic style and attractive persona, amounted to nothing compared to the determination and compassion he saw in the depths of her eyes.

7

Red Ridge Lake featured the type of commonplace camping facilities that called to Kiara's memories of summer camp, and rustic vacations with her family. Pleasantly weathered plank-wood cabins featured step-up porches with wrap around awnings. Amenities included a store, a long, narrow recreational/mess hall and a pair of male and female bath facilities. Trees burnished by the vibrant, fiery birth of autumn rimmed a wide calm lake that perfectly reflected the colors, the puffy white clouds and surrounding mountain peaks. Wood and pine spiced air assailed her senses.

She helped unpack the two vans, then the group broke off into four teams of five and they trekked to their cabins.

Following a quick settling in period, Kiara wandered toward the lake. Canoes were neatly stacked near the shoreline. A sturdy looking dock extended several feet into the water. Plastic chairs surrounded a deep, rock-lined fire pit. Next to that resided an endearingly timeworn swing set.

The wooden structure, with thick chain links and a pair of wooden seats, called to a child-like part of her soul. Besides, after the non-stop cacophony of traveling for hours with teenagers, a touch of solitude is exactly what her spinning mind needed in order to reboot.

So Kiara sat down at the swing and pushed off.

Delighted, she pumped her legs and the lake climbed toward her then filled her vision, receding when momentum sent her backwards. The freefall flipped her stomach lightly and tickled her insides. A cool wind kissed against her skin.

She slowed when footsteps crunched on the leaf and needle strewn path of gravel behind her. She turned and butterflies erupted when Ken approached.

A whole different type of freefall took place.

"I wanted to make sure you hadn't run away," he greeted, a teasing smile curving his lips.

She tried not to stare at that perfect, tempting mouth and instead, feigned offense. "You have that little faith in me, eh?"

He stepped into the scuffed and worn spot of dirt behind her and settled his hand against the small of her back. She nibbled on her lower lip as he gave her a push.

The motion sent her gently forward, and then she glided right back to him. He pushed again.

"I have faith in you." He left it at that. "The sundry shop is still open for business in case you're hungry."

Kiara chuckled. "After all the junk food we consumed during the trip? I won't be hungry for days."

She soared back to him, close enough that their gazes met when she turned to look at him. Close enough that she could glean the flecks of gold that highlighted his dark brown eyes.

He pushed; Kiara flew.

"This is a gorgeous setting," she offered starting to tingle, and tremble.

"Um-hmm. Lakes and swim-time never fail to get kids to sign up for mission trips. They don't care how cold the water is."

"Not me. I'm not a fan of ice-swimming."

"When you see the shower facilities, you might change your mind."

Kiara swung a bit more. Sunlight burnished the world to a molten hue of gold. Rich shades of green, red and orange illuminated the waving scrub grass and surrounding trees.

"Can I ask you a question?" he asked.

"Sure."

"I noticed the point in Little Women when you turned inward. You stopped bubbling the minute Marmee March told Meg not to worry so much about being the belle of the ball as maintaining her strength of character. Do you mind my asking why that scene in particular seemed to hit you so hard?"

His question struck against the crux of Kiara's deepest inner-dilemma—one she tried desperately to avoid confronting. To compensate for self-doubt and insecurity, Kiara took comfort in control, especially with regard to relationships. She called the shots with men who fell into easy admiration. Right now though, she depended on Ken, on winning his interest, and not just physically. She wanted something *more*. Something he offered that left her feeling not just beautiful, but fulfilled.

This means something, a voice inside her said, *but you're not the one in control. Neither is Ken. It's out of both your hands. Instead, your fate resides in the steady possession of a loving, heavenly Father. Rest easy in that truth.*

Kiara swung her legs slower and slower,

decreasing her levitation, but continuing to swing.

"The scene kind of hits home," she finally said. "Especially as I find myself mixing and mingling with teenagers."

"Why'o that?"

She came to rest, but Ken pushed her just slightly, giving her the freedom of flight, of movement, while she considered how to answer.

"I've been Meg. I've been the wallflower who bloomed. But Meg believed in herself enough to give up fancy trappings and rely instead on her strength of character. I'm not sure I possess that kind of courage. I've clung to vanity-centered ideals for too long, I suppose. I've worked hard to fit in, and finally I succeeded. Problem is that kind of success is a double-edged sword. That pathway, once you start to follow it, is hard to leave."

In an unexpected, graceful motion, Ken caught her swing by the chains. He held her in place, suspended backward, with nothing but a cushion of air between them. All at once Kiara went dizzy and hyper-focused, tempted once more by that full, supple mouth, and the satiny-looking fall of his thick brown hair as he leaned over her. He was close enough to touch. In this moment, she wanted nothing more than to do just that.

"Some time, at some point, I'd like to hear more about that, Kiara. I'd like very much to know how you became the woman you are."

She looked at him steadily. "I'd bore you to tears. It's nothing extraordinary."

"All present evidence to the contrary." He set her gliding once again and Kiara's stomach performed a sparkling fall-away. She delighted in his words but forced herself to brush them aside before they could take root and sway her into believing he saw richness to her spirit. After all, it was part of Ken's persona to be gracious and encouraging.

But he continued, and those arguments splintered to shards when he said, "You're moving forward in directions that are not only admirable, but eye-opening—not just for you, most likely, but to everyone who's part of your life—don't hold to what other people see, or expect of you. Be who you are. And while you're at it, create the best version of yourself you can imagine. The only question, with the only relevance that matters, is this, Kiara: Who are you *now*?"

When she sailed back his way, he caught the chains of her swing once again and whispered in her ear, "I believe in you."

With that, he released her on a push, sending her on another dizzying spin of sensation. He walked away, retracing his steps up the path to the cabins and mess hall. She swung to a stop then sat in silence for long moments after he left, absorbing, shivering in a way that had nothing at all to do with the cool of the encroaching night.

∽∾

Since the Woodland team ate dinner on the road, Kiara didn't have to worry about food—or cooking and cleaning—once they settled into camp. To finish off day one, the entire troop met in the recreation hall, which doubled as the eating area. The building featured a huge kitchen and lines of cafeteria-style tables. While Ken conducted a brief info-session to map out tomorrow's schedule and the KP itineraries,

Kiara noticed even the most energetic teens leaned their heads and elbows on the tabletops and yawned frequently.

In conclusion, they toured the campgrounds and became familiar with its layout. They entered the bathhouse en masse to check out the facilities, which were empty for now. The kids performed a unilateral grumble when viewing the space. Sure enough, Kiara found out Ken's earlier comments about the condition of the showers hit the mark.

Sliding back a white vinyl curtain Amy poked her head into a stall. Kiara peeked in along with her, and cringed. Couldn't help it.

Amy said it for them both: "OK, seriously? This is so far beyond the word gross."

Peripherally Kiara noticed Ken standing in the doorway, watching; he seemed to be waiting on her reaction.

In honesty, she tended to agree with Amy, who made a valid point. To her credit, though, Amy didn't whine. She made her comment, and then shrugged, looking at Kiara for reaction as well.

Attempting stalwart behavior despite black mildew splotches on the yellowed calking, despite the peeling floor and chipped wall tiles Kiara said, "Yeah. Gross covers it pretty well." A clean-looking plastic floor mat hung on the wall next to the stall. Kiara unhooked it and dropped it to the floor inside the shower. "This will help. Besides—at least it's a shower, with hot water. We're staying in a cabin with beds and clean linens. For now, we're a few steps ahead of the family we're here to help, right? And for us, it's temporary. For them, it's constant."

Just like that, she found herself the center of

attention. Mere words stirred comprehension of what they were there for, along with a renewed perspective. Amy's eyes brightened. She nodded and pulled the curtain back into place, saying, "Yep. You're right."

A few more murmurs of reluctant agreement followed as they gathered outside. When Kiara passed Ken, leading her four lady delegates to their assigned cabin, he slid his hand against hers and he gave it a squeeze. His smile spread slow and sure, like sunlight breaking through a thick bank of clouds.

"And to think you were once intimidated," he said.

8

Sunlight beat onto Kiara's exposed neck, the air thick, laden by an unusual degree of humidity. She yanked away an obstructing line of overgrowth and bramble that lined and overcrowded the front of the Kidwell residence.

"This is gonna take forever," Amy muttered.

"Yeah—but it'll make dinner and shower time feel that much better," Tyler said, ever present and encouraging. Kneeling next to Amy, he pulled weeds as well. Kiara swiped her brow with the back of her hand and watched the twosome move in a neat tandem down the wood-beam border that had just been installed to frame in a small flowerbed.

Kiara smiled at the way Tyler looked at Amy, quietly enamored. Pretty similar, she imagined, to the way she looked at Ken. The thought left her searching for him. Ken stood atop a nearby ladder propped against the roofline, handing up equipment and supplies to a crew that replaced disintegrated tiles.

"It's not that I don't want to help, but, *dang!*" Punctuating her statement, Amy grabbed a handful of tall, leafy sprigs and yanked them free. "This thing is a mini *tree!*"

Tyler gave her shoulder a shove and they laughed.

Kiara piped in, picking up a pair of gardening shears and giving her all to trimming bushes. "I hear that, Amy." Minutes later, she gathered up discarded branches. "Maybe you can think about it this way: Consider the fact that everything we do right now is one less thing Casey has to worry about. Plus, it's not like she has any extra money to spend. She can't repair the roof, or replace those rotted floorboards in the porch. She can't replace kitchen cabinets and lay new flooring. The elbow grease is tough, and sweaty, but it's why we're here, right?"

"Well said, Kiara."

She froze, her arms chock-full of thick, prickly tree branches. A recycle bag stood nearby, tall and half full—completely ignored when she turned, and faced Ken.

"She's brilliant," Amy deduced, not even looking their way while she continued to tug at the weeds and wrinkle her nose at the muddy debris. Her unguarded praise made Kiara's skin flame, because it only served to expand Ken's smile.

She faced him like a statue, roughened bark and pungent leaves punctuating her senses of touch and smell. Ken stepped close and removed the refuse from her grasp. "Let's dispose of these before they end up back on the ground."

Ken stuffed the branches into the recycling bag, then took Kiara's arm and led her away from the activities of the landscaping detail. He walked toward a stack of boxed up shingles that stood on the porch. "Can you help me with some supplies over here on the porch? The contractors need more materials. I was thinking you could hand them up to me while I'm on the ladder."

"Sure," she answered quickly, glad to divert from the fact that she had openly gawked at the man.

"We're nearing the end of the day ahead of schedule." He looked over his shoulder at Tyler, Amy and Carlie. Kiara puzzled over the way he paused. He seemed to be buying time while he retrieved roofing nails, a short stack of shingles and water to replenish the crew. He gathered the supplies rather than handing them over. At length he said, "Kiara, have you ever thought about joining the youth group ministry as a team leader?"

Kiara blinked a few times. "Ah. No."

"You should."

"Me?"

"You."

Flattered by his confidence, she tried to clear her head, and think. Ken's idea took strong, unexpected root, weaving through her mind, thriving, enlivening her spirit. She stammered a bit then tried to call him out on the suggestion, probing his seriousness. "Trust me, I'm nobody's theologian. I can't quote scripture verse for verse, or lead discussions on doctrine, or—"

"Who says you have to? Who says that's even necessary? Knowing the Bible is important, of course, but more important to these kids is someone who leads by example."

That ideal crashed in, obliterating her fast-breaking happiness. "That's definitely not me. I'm the Cosmo girl, remember?" He looked at her for a long, intent moment. Kiara's automatic, teasing smile weakened a bit under his regard.

"I tend to look a bit deeper than that, Kiara. In you, I see much more than a Cosmo girl and a beautiful face. Personally? I think STAGE was tailor-made for you."

OK, that was the last thing she expected to hear.

Really? She wanted to ask.

"Ken…I—"

"These kids need engaging. Someone they want to relate to," he continued, cutting off her disquieted protest. "Someone they admire. Someone who leads them to Christ in the manner by which they live, not just in their words, but in their actions as well. Look around you, Kiara, at what you've helped create. That's *you*. And you have a history of success."

"But…*Ken*…"

Her breath hitched and held somewhere deep in her chest. Kiara's heart thundered; her bones turned fluid. *Because, dang it, the idea pulled at her. Tempted. He honestly thought she was worthy and capable of such a challenge.*

Never had a man made her feel so precious and important. Ken seemed to believe she could be much more in this life than a trophy, a woman to be shown off and admired, yet never taken to heart with true relevance.

Kiara didn't realize she was staring at him, absorbing his words, until Ken leaned in with that mind-dizzying smile, and kissed her cheek. "By the way?" he murmured, "You might want to be careful."

Careful? Huh? His voice, low and smooth, danced across her skin in a flutter of sensation.

"The way you said my name just now? Hit me harder than a long, deep look into your eyes. Thanks for leaving *Pastor* off this time."

Before Kiara could stammer out a response, he turned, making ready to rejoin the rooftop crew. Kiara floundered, in a number of ways. "Ah, didn't you need my help?"

Ken looked over his shoulder. "Nah. That was a

diversionary tactic. I just wanted to talk to you alone for a minute."

He moved back, leaving her to stare, and melt, and *wonder*.

Late that afternoon everyone returned to camp. Taking a break before dinner preparations, individual teams adjourned to their cabins. Finally, Kiara's spotty cell phone reception decided to play nice, and she received a series of delayed text messages. The first one came from Daveny, just wanting to check in. That left Kiara smiling as she tumbled flat into bed with a delicious sigh, letting the girls blow off steam. Giggles echoed off the walls, and a pillow fight ensued—as did a simultaneous session of the Scoop, Info and Gossip Society.

Content, thoroughly happy, Kiara tuned out the chatter and paged through a couple more messages from friends, then a final, more surprising entry from Drew.

Miss u. Hear thru the grapevine u left 4 a church trip? Is that 4 real? Mission work over Paris? Whats up w/that? LOL. Fill me in. Ur silent these days. Why?

Interested in deflecting the skeptical undercurrent of Drew's missive, she decided to fill him in promptly. Ignoring the other messages, she started to type a reply.

Dont b so surprised! Our pastor knows how to motivate. Hes awesome n experienced w/ projects like this. Im in PA w/the youth group helping a family of four get back on their feet. Doing landscape and basic home repair. Great program! Im inspired! TTY when I get back.

A stuffed yellow duck whizzed through the air, zipping across Kiara's prone form. The unfortunate, battered toy was the object of a game of keep-away.

Squeals filled the air, followed by a chase full of thunder-feet. Did these kids *ever* get tired? Increasingly able to deflect the ruckus of exuberant teenage girls, Klara clicked send, and her lips quirked into a private grin.

Don't be so surprised I'm on a mission. I'm inspired. He's awesome…

One thing was certain: Her eyes were opening up to a whole new world, and her joy and contentment within that world, while startling, could not be denied.

9

An hour later, as dinnertime approached, Ken came upon Kiara in the mess hall. Alone, she prepped the evening's entrée. The sight of her made him smile.

Standing in profile, she laid out defrosted Tilapia in a line. Before her were three bowls. Her motions as expert as any New York sous chef, she coated the fish in egg, dipped the piece into flour until it was dusted white, then flipped it repeatedly and methodically until bread crumbs formed a light coating. Setting the complete section of fish on a baking tray she hummed and swayed, unaware of his presence.

Deliberately covert, he moved to join her. Ken realized now why she didn't hear him, and why her body moved in time to a beat. She tuned into an iPod, a set of telltale white ear buds tucked into place. Ken wondered. Was he now, officially, the only person on the planet without one?

He wanted to touch her. He wanted connection. He craved her attention and the return of affection that rose up fast and overwhelmed him—but what about *her*? A feminine mystique enveloped her, and enticed.

She turned her back for a moment, dialing the oven to 350 degrees. That's when he stepped up and checked out the meal progression. By design, when she returned to the counter, she came up against his solid, waiting form. She yelped in surprise.

Ken settled his hands on her shoulders, and came upon skin so dewy soft he found himself looking at her bare arms, savoring their warmth and supple texture. Moisturizer. Of course she would moisturize her skin. The thought of massaging cream onto her arms, her shoulders and legs, left him decidedly lax in the concentration and focus department.

"Ken...ah...hello there..."

Her voice, the perfect combination of smoke satin that haunted his mind, took on a new measure of huskiness. Her smile trembled a bit—just like his fingertips, which twitched in a longing to skate against her arms, and caress her.

Thus, his plan to take her by surprise utterly backfired. Now he was the one who came away jostled and hot-wired. It was one thing to have the goal of getting under her skin. It would be quite another figuring out what to do once he got there. *If* he got there. Why did he brave this exercise? Why did he long so urgently to move into her life?

Because within her he sensed passion for life—joy and most important of all, an authentic heart.

"Tilapia happens to be a favorite of mine," he finally said.

She looked down quickly, her cheeks an appealing hue of pink. "Glad to hear that."

Ken felt the way her body tightened, hated the way her eyes shuttered and her focus remained on everything else but him. In a way, he understood her shy avoidance—heady atmosphere ranged around them, intensifying each time they came together.

So he couldn't resist. He grazed his knuckles against her cheek and came away aching. Cheeks of satin—just like the skin of her arms. "Relax, Kiara."

"Easier said than done," she murmured.

Curious he lifted her iPod from where she had resettled it on the counter. He cycled through her play list and hummed with approval.

"One Republic, Creed, David Gray, Mercy Me, Coldplay—" She blushed further and tried to swat his hand away but he dodged the effort and continued reciting: "The Fray, Five for Fighting…they're *great* by the way."

"You *know* them?"

Kiara's surprise ignited a nipping bite of frustration. She was surprised because he knew and enjoyed current music as well as Christian offerings. In a way, she reflected the attitude of most of his parishioners, especially since Barb's death. They saw him as something beyond a man with standard, relatable likes and dislikes, pains and joys.

And needs.

Ken stilled and fought back that dose of negativity by taking in a breath and observing a silence that caused Kiara's brows to pucker. He took a chance on revelation. "I don't know why it surprises people so much that I'm a part of the world I live in. Part of its culture." Absent of forethought he fingered the electronic device. He waited, hoping she might be curious enough—and *care* enough—to pick up the threads he laid out. He wished she would pursue a more personal, more meaningful conversation.

"I didn't mean to offend you." Earnest eyes and genuine regret shaded her words. Ken shook his head and returned the iPod, wanting to rail at how formal, how forced her words sounded.

He kept quiet and started to turn away but fought the leaving. He longed for her to somehow understand him and his life. Was that even a possibility?

She touched his arm. "You wanted to say something. I wish you would."

Her gesture stayed Ken's exit. He expelled a breath. "Oh, boy."

He looked her straight in the eye, thinking, *you wanted her unguarded, right? That's what appealed to you most about this moment, right?* Well, apparently this was his chance, the answer to a prayer.

"Are you sure?" he asked.

She took a moment. Ken watched as she steeled herself a bit. But she nodded.

He kept his tone low. Soft. "First of all, you didn't offend. You reacted in a way that made me want to make something clear, that's all."

"What's that?"

He moved very close. Perhaps leading her forward based on his own strident emotions was just this side of aggressive, but Ken didn't want to fight himself any more. God's hand was here; he just needed to take hold, and have faith.

So he invaded her space to such a degree that she had to look up. Her eyes were wide—and alluring. She didn't step back, or away, so neither did he.

"I believe in being an engaged part of the world around me, Kiara. In fact, I enjoy it. John Muir once wrote that we should be in the world, not just on it. That philosophy hit home with me. I believe that's what God wants for all of us. No matter what our calling. After all, that's why we're here, right?"

Her mouth opened, as if she wanted to respond, but she remained silent, looking at him intently. He reached out, stroked a fingertip against her cheek once more. He couldn't get enough of the sensation that slid through his body when he touched her.

"Secondly I want you to think about something for me."

"What's that?"

The cadence of her voice ignited a dance of sparks through his bloodstream. Ken looked nowhere else but her eyes. "Think about finding a way to see past me being a pastor and understand there's more to me than church leadership. That would mean a lot, Kiara."

Not waiting on an answer, he ended the moment. "I'm going to rally our crew to start helping set up for dinner. The food looks great."

"It certainly does," came the voice of Maggie Voorhees. She stood at the entry of the mess hall, and moved slowly forward. "I wanted to be sure Kiara found everything she needed to cook the fish. Everything okay?"

Startled, a shower of cold, prickling ice danced through Ken's body. Openly curious, openly suspicious of the blatantly cozy stance he presently shared with Kiara, Maggie joined them, but quickly moved her features into smoother, friendlier lines.

"Can I help with veggies? Or some rice, maybe?"

Kiara drifted, as unobtrusively as possible, back toward the baking tray. "That'd be great. Perfect timing, actually. I'm sure the oven has preheated by now, and these won't take long to cook."

Ken prepared to take his leave, figuring it would be for the best. They shared a lingering look before he turned away, and he swore he could feel her eyes on his back when he pushed open the squeaky screen door and walked outside.

જન્જ

The following day, Kiara yanked weeds. She chopped back excess evergreen branches. She worked herself to a wicked extreme, consumed by her thoughts.

Of *course* Pastor Ken—*Ken*, she corrected firmly—possessed a multitude of facets and layers as a person. He was obviously more than a pastor, active and attuned to his time and place in *culture*. Of *course* she realized that truth.

A convicting voice spoke up, though: *Then why is it so difficult for you to call him Ken? Why is it so uncomfortable for you to let this wonderful, textured person into your heart—not as a preacher, but as a man?*

She knelt in the front yard, before the Kidwell's freshly soiled flowerbed. Day two was on the wane, and niggling thoughts kept playing and replaying through her mind. She dove into hard labor and the process of planting a variety of annuals and perennials. She paused to swipe beads of sweat from her forehead while she studied the gradually improving grounds.

Kiara answered that inner voice while she resumed working. *The situation with Ken is difficult because letting him inside my life would open up an even more personal channel between the two of us at a point when I don't know if I'm right for him. Plus, I've just uncovered a whole new element to exploring a relationship with him—parishioner response. Oh, she played silent and uninvolved while we finished up dinner preps last night, but Maggie's intrigue and almost disapproving suspicions only affirm the fact that there are members of Woodland Church who would be disconcerted by romantic developments in the life of their shepherd—no matter how innocent or above-board.*

Especially with a woman like me.

Stop trying to handle *this, Kiara,* came that irritatingly irrefutable voice of reason.

She'd always been attracted to Ken, ever since meeting him years ago at the church renovation project. Married at the time, he became a safe point—a man she could admire from afar, and even learn from, without risking her heart.

Or so she had thought.

Times had changed. His single status left Kiara floundering now—to the point of being uncharacteristically on edge. Acutely aware. Thing was, he knew it. She recognized as much by the way he kept tabs, and stayed near—but not *too* near. He paid close attention, stoked a fever then slid tantalizingly back, allowing her to absorb. Beneath it all simmered heat. Desire. An inviting, although unnerving, degree of tension.

Kiara's volunteer team continued to focus on landscaping. The roof now restored, Ken's team focused on interior renovations side by side with a crew of contractors from local businesses and churches who donated their time. Margaret Voorhees and her husband led Woodland's third and fourth teams in reshaping the backyard.

A hand glided against Kiara's shoulder, warm and large, stirring a jolt. She knew it was him. She recognized his touch.

"You doing OK?" Ken asked. He didn't look at her. He looked instead at a freshly prepped flowerbed now set for flowers.

"Great," she answered—too quickly.

He grinned at Amy who pulled off her work gloves and paused for a long gulp of bottled water. Ken directed his next comment to her, not Kiara. "Well,

I'm not one for micro-managing so I'll leave you to it, but I wanted to say it looks really good out here. I'm headed back inside."

"See ya, Pastor Ken," Amy answered breezily, recapping her drink. She continued to pull away the last of the overgrowth.

Kiara returned to work as well, but hang it all, Ken had her chasing after her tail these days.

"Miss Kiara?" A pair of identical twin pixies, Casey Kidwell's twin daughters, stepped up and stood near her side.

"Hi, Amber! Hi, Alyssa!" Matching, gap-toothed smiles were her return greeting. "How are you?"

"Good," came the unison answer. The little girls shared a quick glance then Alyssa spoke. "Can you and Miss Amy come to our room for a sec? We got somethin' to show you."

Amy looked up, and Kiara gave a slight shrug and nodded. Amy replied, "Sure, guys. What's up?"

"Nothin.' Just a surprise," answered Amber. She pulled Kiara's hand while Alyssa grabbed Amy by the arm.

Inside, at the far end of the hallway, plastic sheeting trapped the dust and floating debris where the more substantial outer wall demolition was taking place. Soon this area would become a third bedroom for the house. Presently, a second bedroom was shared by the three children, the space divided in half by a colorful if threadbare quilt to give the oldest child, Phil some semblance of privacy. Before the week was out, though, Phil would have his own room. The girls would continue to share, following an upgrade and proper maintenance to the room where they now stood. Ken worked outside the doorway, pulling down drywall and hauling away litter.

Oblivious to the construction chaos, Amber said, "It's right in here. C'mere."

Kiara shared an expectant look with Amy, waiting while the girls dug through a large plastic tub where they stored a few of their possessions during this temporary displacement.

At last, they pulled out two small, cloth pouches and handed one to Kiara, and one to Amy. Puzzled, Kiara opened the one from Amber. She tipped the contents into her palm and out tumbled a colorful, beaded bracelet. The beads were the kind of tiny, rainbow colored trinkets to be found in any dime-store jewelry making kit, and her throat swelled. Alyssa tended to Amy; Amber, meanwhile, took custody of Kiara's bracelet, pulling the elastic band just wide enough to slip it onto her wrist.

"We made 'em on our own. It was fun." Amber turned Kiara's wrist this way and that, studying the placement and shine of the piece. "Lots of stuff is fun now. Mommy smiles all the time now. She hasn't done that in a long, long time. It's because of you guys—we just know it. This is a gift. It's to say thank you. OK?"

Kiara bit her trembling lower lip. No use. Tears still filled her eyes, and she tried to blink them back so as not to embarrass the little girls. Meanwhile, the twins waited and watched them with expectant eyes, smiling with the humble joy of giving someone a present.

Thank God for Amy, who, though choked up as well, chimed right in. "You guys are awesome. This is gorgeous. I'm not taking it off."

"Me either. And you certainly don't need to do this to thank us, but we'll treasure these bracelets.

Always. Thank you."

Kiara and Amy scooped them into hugs, and shared a happy laugh as the foursome tumbled into a bit of a heap on the floor. From the corner of her eye, while Amber and Alyssa trounced and giggled, Kiara caught sight of Ken who hefted several large chunks of busted up drywall and dumped them into a nearby wheelbarrow. He looked keenly into her eyes, and then the corners of his mouth lifted, forming into a smile that heated her body—and her soul.

A short time later Kiara returned outside, seeking a private spot where she could release some small portion of the emotions that roiled through her system. At the edge of the backyard, she found what she sought—peace and sanctuary. She leaned against the thick trunk of a ripe-leafed maple tree and tears fell unheeded down her cheeks. She closed her eyes and lifted her face to the sun, letting its warmth bathe her dampened cheeks, her neck and arms.

From behind, a tender touch slid along the length of Kiara's shoulder. This time she didn't even flinch. She didn't even open her eyes. Dang it. Why did the man always happen upon her when she was most exposed? In general, she didn't cry—now it seemed that crying was a way of life. She willed herself to remain lax. Ken stepped close and stroked an errant tear onto his fingertip. "Amy was getting ready to send out a search party. She was pretty emotional, too."

Kiara's senses swirled. She couldn't find her focus or get to a safe, even center. Did she even want to? Kiara looked up, and came upon Ken's warm, penetrating gaze. With a quirk of his lips, he handed her a handkerchief, which caused her to laugh in a shaky manner and inform, "This makes two. I never returned…"

"Never mind that," he interrupted.

She wiped her eyes and absorbed the vibration of intimacy they shared. "I just need a minute."

Silence fell while a breeze set branches chattering. "I saw what happened—what the girls did for you and Amy." Ken held her shoulders, furthering a connection that pulled her irrevocably forward, yet scared her as well. She wrapped her arms against her midsection, bracing against tremulous and varied emotions—gratitude, humility, and beyond all else, a longing that flowed straight from the core of her to Ken in wave after wave.

"Stop fighting so hard," he whispered. "I warned you this trip would stir up changes. That statement wasn't just directed at the kids."

He drew her in and rubbed her back, swaying a bit as he held her close. The tears stopped, but Kiara dissolved on a sigh of pure contentment. Something foreign and completely unexpected broke free inside of her, and then took over. "Those little girls have nothing, but they made gifts. And here's the thing—they didn't say they were grateful for *things*—for their new, improved room, a prettier house, or a better way of life. They never once even mentioned those things. They made these bracelets because they were grateful to us for making their mom smile again. They did it for what we've done for Casey, not what we're doing for them. Destitute as they are, that's where their heart is. That selflessness did something to me, Ken. It makes me feel so ashamed for all the times I've been me-centered, or greedy."

The words poured out of her; emotions worked free and untangled into a fluid, silky sensation of connection between her, and the man who held her steady—and strong.

"Kiara?" he murmured gently, after a stilling, calm silence moved past.

"Yes?" She happily savored the beat of his heart beneath her cheek. Reluctantly she lifted her head and looked into his eyes. The peace, the all-encompassing love that defined his nature was all right there, in a sea of rich brown that penetrated, and aroused. Her pulse started to race.

"Welcome to God's mission on Earth, angel."

They separated, just as footfalls could be heard from the left. Maggie called out rather stridently, "Ken, you're needed inside…"

Kiara couldn't stifle a sigh, nor avoid the pinpricks of her own self-doubt.

10

That night, after dinner, the kids settled in their cabins, hooked into handheld games, iPods and portable DVD players. Ken, meanwhile, embraced the idea of giving them a few hours of independence and opted for a peaceful, nighttime walk along the shores of Red Ridge Lake.

He had a lot to think about.

Granted, he had asked God for a way into Kiara's heart, but what he'd neglected to consider were the ramifications of what he'd do if ever allowed to inhabit that space.

Ken breathed deep of cool air laced by wood smoke from a blooming campfire. He soothed himself by closing his eyes, and turning his world to black. Instantly, an image of Kiara came to life—vivid green eyes, gorgeous, sexy and charismatic; a devastating smile, willowy stature softened by gentle curves...

And an enormous heart in the process of a God-inspired transformation.

Two very intriguing and appealing sides to a coin. But questions plagued him. Could she be satisfied with him in the long term? Could the woman who inspired offers of jet-set trips to Europe, who enjoyed a glittery lifestyle and active social circle, be content with a minister? A missionary with a quiet, modest life? Kiara was a woman accustomed to successful men of means.

His own success was notable, to be sure, but not on an intrinsic level, or in ways modern culture would embrace.

Demons of doubt had crept into his soul without Ken fully realizing it until now.

The encroaching night dimmed his world as he resumed walking. A half-moon became more vivid with the passing minutes, lending milky light to the surroundings. Lost in thought, he moved along the edge of the shoreline, continuing to ponder. Muffled voices from the fire pit echoed through the quiet atmosphere. Trees stood in inky silhouette. Meanwhile, his heart thudded, a deflated feeling taking charge of his mind while he studied the angles of building a long-term relationship with Kiara.

His pace picked up in response to the disquiet that surged, leading him to…

A sensual shockwave.

Nearing a dock, he came upon Kiara, and his footsteps literally stuttered until he stood at its edge, frozen still, studying her dimly-illuminated outline. She sat at the end of the structure, unguarded and unaware, dipping her feet into the water. She braced on her hands, leaning back to study the star-dusted bowl of a sky.

Ken stepped onto the back end of the dock and moved toward her. The creak of a wooden board beneath his feet alerted her to his approach and she turned. Her smile of welcome eased any hesitance he would have felt at interrupting her solitude. In fact, the power of it slid warm through his turbulent, yearning heart.

"This feels good," she remarked.

"I can imagine." He paused about mid-way down

the dock. "You probably don't want me to interrupt."

"Please do. No worries."

He hesitated, part out of shyness, part out of an honest desire to simply leave her to her thoughts, and the peace of the night. So he fell back onto a touch of humor. "OK, but I might be tempted to continue my recruitment efforts on behalf of Woodland." He stuffed his hands into the pockets of his jeans, wondering why the compulsion to reach out to her hit him with such conquering force.

"I'm up to the challenge." She moved over a tad—just enough to make room for him at the end of the dock.

And God help him through complicated emotions, he literally ached to join her. Ken's steps forward were tentative, but his heart most definitely was not.

"If you're sure…"

"Ken, I'm positive."

Ken. Not *Pastor* Ken. Formalities between them eased day by day, and that fact pleased and assured him.

So he settled next to her, shoulder to shoulder. Her skin was warm, and soft. He looked down at her as she watched the rippling waters of the lake and the silvery moonbeams that sparkled on its surface, reflecting back on her features with an ethereal glow. He slipped off his sandals and set them on the dock, dipping his feet into the lake as well.

"So."

Kiara laughed. "So."

He sidled her a mischievous look. "So I slid a sleeping pill into Maggie's coffee tonight. Hopefully that'll put her out for a couple of hours…"

She spun toward him, obviously shocked. Then

she started to laugh, hard. "I can't believe you just said that!"

"I've known and worked with her for well over a decade. I'm allowed. I honestly adore the woman, but…"

The dangling sentence spurred her on. "But she's protective," Kiara observed, a gentle kindness in her tone.

"Yes she is. Seeing the way you and I interact obviously has her radar working overtime. It's not you; it's the situation. Nonetheless, I'm not going to apologize to anyone for taking the time to be with you."

Kiara tilted her head, watching, and despite the darkness, Ken could almost see the wheels turning in her mind. Whether his words comforted or disquieted, he couldn't quite tell.

"I'm flattered, by the way," she finally said.

The statement came at him out of nowhere, so he drew back from a world of black cashmere and focused instead on reality.

"What?"

She looked his way. "I want you to know I'm flattered by the idea that you think I'm capable of working in the youth ministry."

Ken looked after her, wishing he had a clearer read on her facial features at the moment. "From where I sit, it's obvious. And this wouldn't be *working*. It would be *leading*." She attempted to laugh that comment aside, but he didn't let her. "Remember when we first toured the camp, and saw the bathroom facilities? You aced that tricky situation like a champ. And don't even get me started on the way you've helped unite our group to hard physical labor." He paused. "That said, I'll now officially let the topic rest."

"Promise?" She teased, arching a brow. In the half-light of the moon, her eyes sparkled.

Ken busted her chops right back. "I promise. *Except…*"

"*Except?*"

"Except that watching you and Amy makes me think of what you must have been like at her age. Popular and sparkling—the belle of the ball."

That stilled their sense of levity. Kiara kept smiling, but something in the air between them went taut. Ken wasn't sure what to make of it until Kiara replied quietly. "Nope. Not even close."

"Would you care to elaborate?"

She hesitated for a moment or two, and then shrugged. "Actually, I was the high school wall flower."

Truly surprised, he shook his head. "Sorry. Not buying that one at all."

"It's true. I was a total plain-Jane."

"I can't even imagine."

Kiara nodded. "I lived in Grosse Pointe but what most people don't realize when they hear the words *Grosse Pointe* is that there's a layer of people who don't live the so called luxury, high-end Grosse Pointe lifestyle. There are thousands of families who want the address, the school system, but aren't wealthy, or at all upwardly mobile. That's my story."

He watched her, silent and enthralled.

"My mom and dad moved there for my benefit, and my younger brother's benefit, but we had a modest home. Actually, we had a slightly below modest home, to be honest. The school system opened up opportunities, but as I'm sure you've seen in working with kids, there's a clique culture when it comes to adolescence, and there are perceptions that escalate out of all proportion."

"You weren't the cheerleader? The girl voted most likely to…"

Kiara interrupted with haste. "No. Not in the least. I buried myself in academics. I fought, scraped and bled for any scholarship I could find and ended up at Michigan State. With Daveny. I couldn't afford designer labels, or drive an expensive car like a lot of my classmates. I was beneath notice, so I became invisible. High school was a lonely experience, but that loneliness paid off. It gave me the motivation to get good grades, and get a college education."

"Still—forgive me, Kiara, but—I can't even picture it," he said. "You're certainly not invisible anymore. What changed?"

Water flowed around his feet and calves, silky and softly enticing. An inner heat pushed outward to do battle with the chill of soft breezes and cooling night air.

The woman to whom he attributed the bloom of warmth continued. "Going to college helped open me up. It leveled the playing field, you know? I met all kinds of interesting people, but by the same token, I have to admit to going a little shallow in the process."

They swished their feet and let them float. Occasional fish-jumps in the water beyond added noise to a near perfect silence. Kiara continued. "I started taking my looks more seriously. I worked every second I could to earn enough money to be able to—well I'm ashamed to admit this, especially to you—"

Her words caused him to interrupt. "Why not *me*, especially?"

She looked Ken straight in the eye. Even in the deepening black, he could feel her earnestness, her hesitance. "Because I don't want you to think any the less of me."

"You don't have to worry about that, Kiara. I promise."

She waited a moment before speaking. "Well, I wanted to know what it felt like to fit in. To be a part of the 'A' crowd. I didn't mind working myself into exhaustion if at the end of the rainbow I might be able to pay for the perfect haircut and color—or maybe a bar night with my sorority sisters, or a manicure and pedicure. I studied, I learned, I copied whatever 'hot' styles I could, until ultimately I transformed."

"And people noticed," Ken concluded unnecessarily. After all, how could they not? This woman was exquisite.

Kiara gave him a quick glance then looked away. "I suppose so, yes. But the capper happened when some girlfriends and I, on a total lark, and probably after a couple too many beers at PT O'Malley's, decided to take a flirting class. I found my calling." She laughed; it was the bubbly, appealing laugh that resonated with beauty and all things genuine. "Don't take that completely the wrong way. I wasn't trying to be a diva, but I found the experience to be a way to open up. Lo and behold, I found out I had a personality. After being part of the woodwork for so long, I discovered friends, and socializing. I found if I took care of myself, I wasn't the ghost I had always felt like while I grew up. Thing is, the changes I experienced kind of took hold. I started to appreciate fine things, and fine men, more than I probably should have."

"It's only human to want to be affirmed, Kiara, and—"

"It's a double edged sword." She shook her head. Silvery light shimmered off her smooth, glossy hair, causing Ken to lose focus for a moment. "Once I made a conscious effort to fit in, to mix with people, my life changed—in some ways for the better, but in many ways I lost sight of the things that bring meaning to life. I turned into that stereotypical person who gives more credence to instant gratification and easy, convenient relationships than things that are more substantial." Her sadness caused him to snap-to.

As a pastor, and friend, Ken was compelled to speak up on her behalf. "That's precisely why you're here. Now you're working yourself to exhaustion not for notoriety, or labels and haircuts, but for the betterment of a family that had lost hope. That says just as much about you as anything from your past. OK?"

She went still, and when she looked into his eyes, searching, he felt swept away.

"I went without affirmation for so long that I get sucked in by the attention I'm given. It feels good to be liked by women...desired by men. It's flattering to a hungry spirit like mine. Just like Meg in Little Women."

He moved as close as propriety would allow, wanting only to give her as much support and connected-warmth as possible.

Kiara continued, her voice husky and low. "I realize, probably too late, that I've given away parts of myself that I wish I hadn't. I had no idea how precious the waiting, and the finding, can be. I didn't have faith. I didn't believe I'd ever find a relationship that was strong, and right."

Like this? Ken longed to ask. *Like I feel whenever I'm near you?* He swallowed and grasped just enough of his role as a pastor to say, "I believe we're the composition of *all* the things we experience in the life God gives us."

"But I've been tempted to do things that aren't right, Ken. You've seen that first hand, unfortunately. I've made some stupid choices."

"Welcome to humanity, Kiara Jordan," he teased lightly, giving her a nudge. "And remember, you've grown from what you've experienced. Remember, too, that being *tempted* is worlds away from *surrender*. If you don't believe me, check out that part in the Bible where Jesus is alone in the desert with the Devil himself."

They shared a smile at that.

"What I'm getting at," he continued, "is that the person you are is the result of everything you experience—the good and the bad. Life is about what you do with what you learn and the circumstances God gives you. Have you grown? Have you learned and evolved? As far as I can see, the answer to all those questions is yes." He touched her cheek. "Stop carrying the weight and accept the forgiveness you're given, Kiara. Then, ask yourself this: What would you allow yourself to write on a completely clean slate?"

Her steady gaze stayed with his. Ken tucked an arm around her waist to both build a connection and lend her warmth and support.

Comfort and ease settled between them for a time, until Kiara said quietly, "OK. Your turn."

"My turn?"

"Yep. I want to know how you've managed to keep your life, your church, and your heart together after losing Barb. I think that's an amazing accomplishment."

Ken could only shake his head. "That's a God thing." She waited on him in silence. The quiet wasn't disconcerting, though. Instead, it soothed, and gave him a chance to evaluate, analyze. "Don't doubt for a moment that the loneliness stings."

"I'm sure. Besides, you're preaching to the choir, Pastor." She gazed toward the heavens and he felt her shrug beneath the hold of his arm. "But look at it this way: At least you've known a deep, abiding love. I'm starting to wonder if I ever will. Maybe I'm just not wired to—"

"Nuh-uh. No. Stop that line of thinking, OK? It's just...well...you need to be *ready* for it. I think God's preparing you for that step. You have to be discerning enough to recognize what will, and what *won't* bring you happiness."

"Like Drew," she said.

In the deepest reaches of her reply, he discerned shame; he saw her struggles and wishes, her passions.

"You know, Daveny made an interesting comment at the party after Jeffrey's baptism. She called me the conduit between Jeffrey and God."

"She's right. In that case, she was absolutely right."

Ken gave her an appreciative squeeze, soaking in her loyalty and absolute conviction of heart. "Thanks— but not completely. Remember who else gathered around that baptismal font? A family. A community. That's the conduit to God. You're a very important part of that, Kiara. Daveny's comment was given with the best of intentions, but, well, do you know what it did? It made me realize, not for the first time lately, that there's a distance between me and the people I serve.

Separation. I can't say as I like that."

She turned, waiting on more. Most likely without even realizing it, she came to lean against him a bit more.

Ken continued. "Barb and I were a somewhat insulated pair, not too dissimilar from most married couples, I suppose. Losing her left so many parts of my life empty." He shrugged. "In a way, I realize that's what I've been trying to escape from lately. The missions were, and are, a part of the healing process for me. The missions are vital, and provide for so much good, but by the same token, I can't keep avoiding the life I built at Woodland. I can't avoid God's calling because of a void."

Kiara sighed. "You really did hit the jackpot with Barb."

"I won't deny that. But, to be honest, I have to admit to being naïve about the whole thing."

"How so?"

His shoulder connected to hers briefly when he shifted to watch a night bird cut across the moon. "I've been a part of Woodland ever since I was ordained. First as Associate, then pastor. I was married the whole time, so I guess I've never felt the distance, the intimidation factor. The title of pastor can close people off just as often as it helps to lend comfort and assistance. I always had Barb at my side, though, an anchor and a buffer against feeling like an outsider."

She nodded, obviously waiting for him to continue. Ken gave up a momentary study of the sky to look down at her. *So close,* he thought. And he fought off a strong inner tremble.

"Do you feel like an outsider now?" She finally asked.

"Right this second? No." Frog voices filled the silence. A steady hum of insect life buzzed in his ears. She didn't look away, and neither did he. "Stewardship is the life I'm called to. The mission I've been given not just as a job, but as a calling from God. I'm happy in it. I love what I do."

"It shows. Believe me. It's compelling to watch you in your element."

"Thanks." He paused there, because he wanted her to absorb the genuine appreciation he felt at her compliment. "Still, my position creates barriers of a sort, and I...it..."

She watched intently, waiting. Her curiosity all but engulfed him, but he couldn't quite complete the thought the way he wanted.

Not yet, anyway.

So he concluded, "It dawns on me more and more that the time for mourning, for retreat, is over. God is showing me that truth with increasing frequency."

Unaware of the underlying current of that statement, Kiara replied with a simple and emphatic, "*Good*."

Ken nodded. "I move on, and I cope. That's what Barb would expect, and want. But...it's hard."

He swished his feet slowly across the surface of the water, raising ripples and mild agitation. The mirrored motion of her feet drew his attention, held it fast, left his throat parched, his soul needy.

Parts of me still ache when her birthday comes around each year, or our anniversary, or when I officiate at baptisms for the babies we welcome into our parish. I banked on more years with her than what we were given, but our lives are in God's hands. I'm at peace with that truth, but that peace, that faith, doesn't mean I don't face an ongoing adjustment, or that there isn't pain involved, and questions as to why I had to watch her wither—leaving me, and this world, piece by piece."

He choked up, taking a couple deep breaths to restore himself. Innocently their legs slid against one another, his roughened a touch by coarse hair, hers silky and infinitely smooth. His senses tingled and sparked. He came alive.

"I want that kind of love."

Her words hit Ken like a thunderbolt. He traced his fingertips against her cheeks, then her jaw, murmuring, "You deserve that kind of love, Kiara, so please, don't ever sell yourself short."

Her breathing went unsteady, and he saw her firm up her jaw and blink a couple of times, her eyes flashing even more vividly as moisture built, and receded. Quickly, he shifted emphasis, wanting to give her some comfort and equilibrium. "Right now, the thing I pray for most is that even a trace of the transformations I'm able to help bring about in others rubs off on me, too. God knows I need that mercy."

Silence returned, near perfect, holy in a way. No light pollution hazed the bowl of black above them. No clouds or dimming atmospheric properties spoiled this perfect slice of the stars, moon, galaxies and even the occasional slow-moving satellite and plane. Against the dock, a gentle lapping of water was accompanied by nocturnal life and the rush and rustle of tree leaves and grass reeds. The sounds soothed and calmed. Lent a bit of finality to the night's revelations.

"We should get back to the cabins," he ventured at last. He extended his hand and she accepted the connection. With a gentle tug, Ken helped her stand.

There was just a hairbreadth of air between them, then none at all. Their bodies brushed, their gazes connected. "Just remember that there's beauty in the simplest things, Kiara. Just open yourself up to it, and receive."

11

The walk back was quiet, but unhurried.

Meandering left Kiara with time to think. In fact, almost *too* much time...

Something about Ken's demeanor caused questions to flow, accompanied by a sense of anxiety she couldn't deny, or escape. This moment between them felt unfinished. She sensed hanging threads and wanted them tied up. Resolved.

So, deliberately she slowed her pace. "Ken?" He turned, waiting. "Was there something more you wanted to say to me? Back at the dock?" Kiara waited, hoping for more from him—for anything that might connect her to him more fully.

"No...not really."

On the inside, she wilted. Looking up she did her best to study his shadowed features and came away unfulfilled. A tree-hidden moon shrouded them in a deep black, and she wondered about his true reactions. The only giveaway she could detect was the quick way he averted his gaze.

That prompted her to push. "Please tell me what's bothering you." She wanted to reach out, the urge so strident her body yearned. "Something's on your mind. Maybe I can help. You're always present to everyone else. I'd be honored to be the one to listen and lend support if you need it."

For some reason, Kiara could tell her offer didn't hit the right mark. She realized the fact instantly when Ken sighed, then closed his eyes for a moment, almost as though in prayer. The dim, sporadic light of the night had made them sparkle. She missed that instantly.

Maybe that was part of the problem. Kiara wanted this man—very much—and in the here and now of performing side-by-side mission work, everything between them felt right—uncomplicated and united. Ultimately, though, they would have to return to the world of reality. Kiara, the quintessence of flirt and playful, modern femininity. Ken, the traditionalist, pastor—a man of calling and humble service.

Maggie Voorhees came to mind, and all of a sudden Kiara's mind's eye conjured the image of oil forming a shimmering, but tarnishing rainbow over a surface of pristine water. Dramatic, yes, but a proper mix would never be accomplished. Attraction could provide a lovely sheen of various colors, but over the long haul she'd end up heartbroken when she disappointed him, and he found it necessary to move away.

Insecurity pinned her within a world of doubt. They were simply too different.

A lengthening moment passed in stillness then they cleared the tree line. He stopped short. He nodded in the direction of a nearby birch and they moved toward it, standing beneath its cover of branches. In fact, Kiara was close enough to the trunk that her back came up against the slightly rough bark. He stood before her, tall and lithe. Broad shoulders blocked out starlight and leaves; his features were inked out, but she didn't need light to gather the image of a squared jaw, deep-set eyes brimming with affection, and compassion, the thick tussle of dark brown hair that waved against the back of his neck. Ken was...was...she wanted to use the word seductive—but the words seductive and preacher? Kiara shivered.

At last, he said, "I don't want to leave you with the feeling that I don't appreciate your support."

"I didn't think that." Well, not *exactly*, she added in silence.

"You possess the sweetest heart, Kiara. But, to you I'm a pastor, and you're my parishioner. There's a divide. It's like I was saying. I'm not good at divides. I haven't faced them very often, that is, until—" The words *Barb passed away* went unspoken, but understood. "I feel a distance, a guardedness in the way you talk to me sometimes, the way you intensify, and go formal when I try to reach out. Please, just keep in mind that I'm only a man. I have a vocation, true, but that makes me no different from everyone else."

This was her fault, just as she feared. She would let him down; she would fail him, and he deserved the very best. Even though she didn't think that person would ever be her, Kiara couldn't stop from asking, "What do you need? What is it you're looking for? Please tell me. Not as a pastor. I care about you above and beyond that title. So many people do. You shouldn't feel alone in this."

Ken clenched his jaw. She saw the taut line bloom, even in the moonlight. She was maintaining the divide, and she knew it. But, she felt terrified to step over that final threshold and lose her heart for good.

"You're not *everyone*, Kiara. Not to me."

Confusion and uncertainty started to clear because Ken's words forced her to connect a few emotional dots. There was something unique and powerful about the two of them, and the bonds they discovered. Ken was sounding her out about that fact. In a round-about manner, true, but nonetheless he tried.

She pondered that fact until Ken asked quietly, "Kiara do you trust me enough to let me try something?"

The way he asked the question made her throat go dry. Her pulse raced and a dizzy, wonderful ache slid straight through her, rendering her completely open and receptive. "How could I not?"

He slid his fingers slowly through the length of her hair. Velvety warmth coasted in on the heels of that stirring ache. He brushed his fingertips against her neck and cheeks, cupping her face. She felt vulnerable, but weakness dissolved her bones, melding her spirit neatly to his.

"Close your eyes."

His request, a mere whisper, left her swallowing cotton. He waited on her compliance, his gaze on her face. Even in the night air, she felt the warmth of his eyes, the patience and care that always seemed to motivate him. Her eyes fluttered closed and she tried desperately to remember how to breathe.

A petal-soft whisper of air slid against her mouth an instant before his lips claimed hers. Moist as dew, as silky and sensuous as the night that cocooned them, his kiss caused her head to spin, left her pliant. A pleasured exclamation left her. Just like that, the sense of drifting to the conclusion of this evening without a completed circle—a sense of fulfillment—evaporated into the air, lifting high and away.

He drew her into his arms, but didn't press further. Instead, he simply fed her—passion for passion, intimacy for intimacy—in kiss after warm, giving kiss. The beauty and mastery he poured into the connection knocked any other emotion and memory Kiara associated with love and physicality into total oblivion.

She held fast to his forearms, clung to him. It was either that or she would literally sink to the bramble-and-brush-covered floor of the woods. She could lose herself in him so easily, and so willingly.

The kiss intensified as they fell into the moment, the act deep and exploratory, provocative and open. Their embrace turned radiant and strangely encapsulating. The crackle of a branch jarred them back to reality and the possibility of being discovered. Nothing else moved around them except a soft, cooling stroke of air as they parted.

Wordless, suffering from what seemed to be a mutual case of shell-shock, they left privacy and seclusion behind. They closed the distance to her cabin and Ken tucked her hand securely in his, caressing the back with his thumb.

Once they reached the steps leading up to the door, she kept hold of his hand to halt his leaving and said, "I want you to know something." He waited and she shored up her courage and unshielded her heart just far enough to take a risk. "Ken, I think of you as being much more than just the head of my church. You're a wonderful pastor, yes, but you're a wonderful man as well."

He stepped close and used a slow finger stroke to tuck her hair back. He leaned in close to nuzzle her neck, then her cheek. "Good night, Kiara." He kissed her cheek then moved away. "And thank you." There was such earnestness to the tone of those final words.

"See you in the morning."

"I hope you have sweet dreams."

He turned back in mid-stride. Beneath the yellow light of a nearby security lamp that illuminated the sandy pathway between cabins, she saw him smile, and her chest swelled with happiness. "I think, tonight, that's pretty much a given. You rest well, too, angel."

He disappeared into the night and Kiara stood at the doorway of the cabin, stupefied. Her mouth tingled. She touched it with shaky hands, ran her tongue slowly against her lower lip. She breathed in deep and he surrounded her—scent, warmth and an ache ripe with longing.

As quietly as she could, she pushed open the door and caught herself in a mindless stumble when her sneaker caught on the edging of the threshold. She cringed, waiting for one of the slumbering girls to awaken. Kiara nearly laughed out loud. Her cabin mates rested in silence. Thank goodness.

Well, so much for being the sexy sophisticate. She was transported, operating completely outside of herself. She felt as giddy as any one of the teens with whom she presently kept company. She smiled the whole time she sneaked beneath the covers and tucked in for the night. Over and over again, she played out the kiss. *Their* kiss.

Ken.

He pulsed through her heart like a living thing. She closed her eyes and he was there. And he was in no way, shape or form simply a preacher any longer. She was in love. The return to reality she had been concerned with earlier seemed suddenly distant and misty. She snuggled beneath the blankets trying to make a restless body go still and comfortable.

Ken Lucerne left her believing she had more to offer this world than the male-enchanting looks and willowy, curved frame, which heretofore had been her claim to fame. The idea of such strength of belief thrilled her—but scared her to bits as well.

A fear of heartbreak loomed—so mist-blanketed fears resurfaced, but only for a moment.

Ken longed, and he ached. At the same time, he struck her as being so strong, so sufficient. So Godly.

He's just a man, Kiara.

Daveny's words echoed, helping her grasp anew the truth that Pastor Ken—*Ken*—experienced needs and pains, joys and triumphs like everyone else. He succeeded and failed like everyone else.

The night rang with a silence broken only by the steady breathing of her bunkies. Ken's words rang through her, body and soul.

"Ask yourself this: What would you allow yourself to write on a completely clean slate?"

She already knew the answer. She'd write his name upon it and guard that slate with the entirety of her heart.

At last she dozed, a smile playing on her lips as she drifted off to a deep, thoroughly restful night's sleep.

12

"Kiara, you are *so* cool."

Kiara couldn't hold back an affectionate laugh at Amy's pronouncement. "Takes one to know one, Miss Thing."

Amy dipped a spoon into the potato salad Kiara was creating and scooped out a sample, devouring it with a sigh. "I'm serious. You even make cooking seem chic. Where did you get your top? I love it."

Kiara burst out laughing again at Amy's CD-skip style conversation. "Amy, the next time I'm feeling down in the dregs, I'm calling you, and you're ordered to say exactly those words to me over and over again." With a downward glance, Kiara paid regard to the sleeveless pink microfiber athletic shirt she wore. "I got this at a running shop in Sterling Heights. I'll take you there some time."

"Deal. Seriously, I'd so love to go shopping with you."

The fourth day of the mission trip was drawing to a close. They were past the midway point and the results were remarkable. Backbreaking, but remarkable. Enough camaraderie and trust had been established, enough observations made, for Kiara to comfortably remark, "You know, Tyler sure is enchanted by you. Bonus? He's such a great guy."

Amy shrugged. "He's really nice. I like how he

treats me."

"You should. Believe me when I say that's the whole ballgame," Wanting to pass along as much wisdom as possible to this younger version of herself, Kiara didn't shy away from the role of mentor.

"I feel bad around him though."

"Why's that?"

"Because I know he likes me, and honest, I like him too. I like him just fine. But…" She paused and watched Kiara dice a bit more onion and celery into the mix. "Need more milk?"

"Yeah. Just a little. The secret is making it creamy, and using enough eggs."

Amy poured, and then Kiara mixed.

"You were saying?"

Amy leaned on her elbows, watching the motion of the spoon in the bowl instead of meeting Kiara's eyes. Kiara didn't know much about young adults, but the body language spoke loud and clear. Amy wanted to confess but wasn't sure what to admit, so she diverted parts of herself—like a gaze that would reveal too much.

"It's just that there's this other guy. Mark Samuels. He's kind of, like, spectacular, Kiara." She grinned. "The type of guy I bet you'd have gone for big time back in high school. He's so handsome, and funny, and he's a total jock—captain of the basketball team. He's awesome. Everybody wants to be around him, and, well, he likes me. I even think he's going to ask me to Homecoming."

Dreamy preoccupation left Amy neglecting Kiara's reaction. Thank God. Amy's words convicted Kiara in the worst way. Amy's ideas, and ideals, were carbon copies of Kiara—once upon a time—until Woodland,

and Ken's presence in her life. In an effort to find conformity, acceptance and, yes, pleasure, Kiara knew she had gone shallow in spots, and this conversation with Amy served to amplify that fact.

So Kiara continued the process of transforming. "Amy, if Tyler treats you well, and he cares about you, and you like him, why wait around for a different guy just because he's popular, or a handsome jock? You've got so much to offer, and to match up with someone who recognizes how special you are, is an amazing blessing."

Kiara turned to put a cover on top of the potato salad then walked to the fridge to store it.

"Like you and Pastor Ken?" Dishware bobbled, but Kiara executed a fast recovery, trembling as she safely shelved the salad then turned back around.

There was a deliberate watchful manner to Amy's posture, and then she said, "I'm sorry. I don't mean to be nosy or anything, it's just that I figured since I'm confessing to you, you might want to do the same."

"Pastor Ken?" The words were nothing but a stall maneuver. She didn't know how to react, or what to say to this insightful, keen-eyed young lady.

Amy elaborated. "Last night. The trees."

Kiara's heart lurched. "Yeah."

"I had to go to the bathroom, and the night was so pretty. There were billions of stars. I wanted to go see the lake. I started down the path through the woods, and I, well, I'm sorry, but I saw you and Pastor Ken."

Kiara didn't know what to say.

"Kissing," Amy clarified.

"Oh."

They eyed one another, mutually unsure how to proceed. Kiara felt trapped by the shared knowledge of an event that she had hoped would remain private.

"You really like him," Amy continued. "I could tell that before I saw what I did."

"Amy, I need to ask you, please, to be discreet about what you saw. It was just a kiss, and it was completely innocent, so I don't want gossip to build, not around Pastor Ken. OK? Can I trust you?"

Her expression turned instantly affronted. "I wouldn't hurt you guys. I didn't tell anyone, Kiara. And I won't. I promise. I really like you both."

Kiara crossed through the kitchen and sat down on the stool next to Amy's. Amy flipped her hair over her shoulder and fingered the spoon she still held, studying it. Kiara settled her hand over Amy's to still the nervous fidgeting.

Amy's features went soft. "I went back to bed and you came in a few minutes later. I could tell by your breathing that you couldn't get to sleep right away. Truth is? I envy you finding that kind of a moment. It seemed so perfect, and wonderful."

"Life isn't ever idyllic, OK? Understand that Ken misses his wife, very, very much. And, in truth, I don't know that I'm the best person to fill that kind of a role in his life."

"Kiara?" she paused. "You're awesome. How can you doubt that? Like, *ever*?"

Quite easily, she wanted to say, but Amy's plaintive, emphatic decree softened Kiara's heart and her determination to turn away from the onslaught of emotion Ken stirred.

The screen door of the mess hall squeaked open, and the guys stormed in, laughing boisterously, colliding with one another on purpose, and preparing to toss a football across the kitchen area, until...

"Guys—food. Don't mess around the food."

Ken entered the hall and herded the gang to a seating area where they were scheduled to reconfirm the delegation of table set up and cleaning assignments for the following day. Kiara spared him a grateful look for his intervention, and he gave her an understanding nod. Kiara tucked a piece of aluminum foil across the top of a tray full of fruit selections she had cleaned and arranged just before her conversation with Amy had begun.

Understanding the need for their interlude to conclude, Amy left the stool and stretched, making a happy sound as she sifted her fingers through her hair. "I call shower!" she sang.

Kiara launched into action; nightmares that featured icy jets of water danced through her head. She gave her newfound confidante a mock glower and literally jogged toward the exit. "Think again, Miss Thing. I'm pulling rank. I crave hot water. For five measly seconds I need hot water! I'll be out in a flash. You can even time me."

"Kiara!" Amy bellowed, chasing after her at full-bore. "No fair!"

The sound of Ken's laughter tickled the skin along the back of Kiara's neck, and danced against her senses as she and Amy charged from the mess hall.

13

The mission trip didn't conclude with a big-reveal style television moment; however, the community reactions, the humble, overwhelming gratitude, remained just as powerful, and just as touching to Kiara.

A farewell breakfast concluded the agenda in Pennsylvania. Afterwards, no sooner did a round of hugs from the Kidwell family end, than they started all over again. Everyone seemed reluctant to part. A new circle of love began with each communion; the Kidwell's happiness turned into a blanket that wrapped around the entire mission team just as tight and warm as their arms. In particular, Casey Kidwell's voice quavered with emotion that laced her repeated words of thanks and praise, not just to the workers, but to the God who had brought everyone together.

On departure, a quiet, somewhat somber mindset colored Kiara's world. The Woodland team began its return trip to Michigan with everyone tired, quiet, and introspective. Still overcome by the outpouring, the teen volunteers spent a good portion of the drive home in what she felt sure was a prayerful, thoughtful silence.

Attempting subtlety, she glanced over at Ken. One hand rested on the steering wheel, the other rested on the divider between them. Kiara was sorely tempted by the image of strong, perfectly muscled forearms lightly dusted by hair that she now knew by touch was as soft as satin. She longed to reach out, to touch him and reconnect. Instead, she held back. Discretion kept her in place, but yearning remained a persistent ting that struck against her heightened nerve endings.

One by one, Ken dropped off their travel companions. When they reached Kiara's apartment, he parked the van, turning to her. They were alone now, confined within the intimate space of the vehicle, surrounded by warmth, dim light and the vibrating purr of the engine.

"I miss you already," he said.

The heartfelt words emboldened her to take the initiative and move forward. She touched his face, her fingertips memorizing each subtle curve, dip and plane. She glided her hand against his neck and drew him close, seeking to indulge a need which had consumed her from the start of the voyage home. Understanding at once, he wrapped an arm around her and she sank into a kiss so sweet, so potent, she went pliant against him.

"I know how you feel. Will we see each other soon? When we…I mean…what will happen…?" Kiara couldn't meet the power of his eyes when she felt such uncertainty. She didn't want to see anything within their depths that might warn of hesitance, or worse yet, doubt. "I wanted—and waited for—this moment for the entire trip."

Even in the darkness, his smile could be discerned. "Me, too. And it was well worth the wait."

Kiara looked up at him shyly, but ventured forth into trickier territory. "Please know that I don't want to make anything awkward for you or uncomfortable at

Woodland."

"Kiara, it's fine. Let's just take it step-by-step as far as revealing ourselves goes. There's no reason to think people won't be thrilled for us."

"Day by day."

He nodded. "Day by day."

She paused, burdened by the secret she knew she needed to share—especially given this conversation. "I have to tell you—"

"What?"

Kiara paused again. "Amy saw us."

"The kiss. In the woods."

She nodded. "Remember that branch that snapped and popped?"

Ken ducked his head in a gesture both endearing and boyish. "I remember." Then his gaze returned to hers, full of heated intensity. "In fact, I remember everything about that moment, angel. Everything."

"You're not worried."

"Not a bit. First, I think Amy'll keep quiet. She looks up to you and wouldn't hurt you."

"Or you," Kiara assured further.

"Come here."

He didn't wait for her to comply. Instead, Ken drew her snug against his hard, warm chest. With restrained hunger, his mouth claimed hers and she gave herself over to a moment of loving joy. She trusted him completely, so she tucked her head into the crook of his shoulder, cradled safe and perfect into a spot of his body and soul that felt like it had been designed for her by God.

Instead of an abrupt, jarring break, Ken ended their connection by soothing degrees. Kiara's heart raced as his lips moved from her mouth to glide smoothly against both cheeks, then to trail against her neck until at last they shared one last, lingering kiss.

With typical, thoughtful chivalry, he hauled her suitcase out of the rear storage area of the van then carried it into the entryway of her apartment. He turned to say goodbye. Before leaving, though, he enfolded her in a hug so snug and eloquent Kiara wanted to sink into the sensation for good.

"Thank you for being the face of Christ to the Kidwells', Kiara. In word and in deed. Your commitment made a huge difference in their lives." He traced a lone fingertip against the underside of her chin, using the subtle gesture to lift her gaze to his. "I'll see you at services tomorrow."

She nodded. Along came an impulse she couldn't possibly ignore. She lifted her hand and allowed her touch to linger against his cheek, then his strong, square jaw. A silence lingered between them before she concluded strongly, "I'll see you then."

∂∞

"Hey! Welcome back, stranger! I missed you!"

"Me, too, Dav! I looked for you at church yesterday."

Kiara hugged her best friend tight. Daveny, meanwhile, all but thrust her through the doorway of her office and into the chair in front of her desk. Kiara was starting to actually harbor a fear of that hideously innocent-looking chair.

"I know, right? Jeffrey and Collin are both under the weather. I had to pull nursing duty, times two, and I'm awfully afraid I'm on borrowed health time." They shared a grin. "So! Tell me all about it!"

Kiara snorted. "Not until I decompress. I swear, teenagers have more energy and stamina, and exist on less sleep, than any living organism I know of!"

Daveny chuckled. "When did you get in?"

"Saturday night. I literally dumped my suitcase in the laundry room of my apartment, still stuffed with grimy, smelly clothes, then I showered—in *hot* water, praise God—for almost a half hour before collapsing into bed. I didn't wake up until the alarm rang. I rolled into church, on time—will miracles never cease—and then returned home for another lengthy sleep session that ended with me waking up just in time to get to work. How's that for a hero's return home?"

Daveny laughed with what Kiara felt was just a bit too much glee. "I take it you're exhausted?"

"Times ten, yes, but in the best way. It was awesome, Dav. I can't get over how much a week of our time helped these people—and gave them a new lease on life. To see their faces, to see the hope our work left behind, makes every ache and every lost hour of rest *so* worth it."

Let that be enough, Kiara thought in a rush. She even started to stand, knowing full well that a bevy of work awaited. Perfect excuse to retreat—er—leave.

Please, oh, please, don't ask about Ken, she pled in silence. *I'm so drained and vulnerable right now I have no defenses left against what I feel. Don't ask about Ken. Don't ask about Ken.*

"And how did my favorite pastor hold up?"

Dang. She asked. And just hearing his name, just thinking about him, betrayed Kiara to her best friend. In an instant, she knew Daveny registered her reaction—the flight of heat that slid smooth and fast up her neck, and cheeks. Kiara diverted her softened eyes, knowing evasion was in vain.

As expected, Daveny wasted no time calling her out, either. *Figured.* Kiara had done the same thing to Daveny a time or two during the course of their friendship—especially when Daveny fell hard, and irrevocably, for Collin Edwards.

"Are you going to sit back down, or do I need to get the restraints?"

Kiara glared. Daveny shrugged. Then, she even *grinned.*

Relenting, Daveny leaned forward, ignoring the photos and layout plans covering her desk. "Consider this a 'me returning the favor' moment. After all, you've done the same for me, now haven't you?"

Kiara sank into the chair and sighed. Every bit of bravado evaporated from her blood stream.

"I'm in trouble."

"Honey? I figured that one out solo. *Talk* to me."

Where to start? What to say? At length, Kiara figured the truth might serve her well.

"OK. You want flat out? I'll *give* you flat out. Daveny, no man has ever impacted my waking thoughts, my dreams. No man has ever forced me to look so long, and so hard, at who I am, and who I want to become. No man's touch has ever worked me over like this. You know me. I can take or leave an attractive man, and I've done both on more occasions that I'd care to admit anymore. Well this isn't casual. This isn't something frivolous, or something to fill time. This is real. This is leagues different from anything I've ever felt before, and it's miles away from my comfort zone. He fills a hunger I didn't even know I had."

The words spilled free. She couldn't stop them. Didn't want to any longer. Kiara lost the will to fight.

Meanwhile, Daveny listened; she nodded, seeming to know exactly what Kiara meant.

"He fills your spirit," Daveny said at last. "Ken brings you close to himself, and close to a God you're beginning to relate to on a much more personal level, Kiara. He's helping you discover the very best of yourself. That's a beautiful thing. Embrace it."

"Until he leaves me, or realizes our two-plus-two doesn't exactly make four when it comes to the two of us becoming a couple."

Daveny reared back. "What on earth do you mean by that?"

"Oh, come on. Do the math! When the equation of Kiara plus Ken patterns down to its conclusion, I just don't see a way for a man like him, and a woman like me, to make a relationship work." Daveny seemed about to speak up, but Kiara shook her head in a silent request for Daveny to hear her out. "I'm way too different from him. Most of all, I'm not *Barb*. I could never fill her role. She was tender and soft—a born nurturer. I'm the sassy, playful modernista."

Daveny studied her for a long, hard moment. Seemed a perfect point in the conversation for Kiara to execute a swift change of subject. "Anyway, enough of all that. Tell me about Sir Jeffrey. How's my baby boy been, other than recovering from a bug?"

That did the trick. In an instant Daveny turned completely maternal—all happy, proud and glowing. Vicariously Kiara shared her joy. "Oh, he's up to his usual tricks—sleeping, eating, and cooing. C'mere. Let me show you the latest pictures."

Truly eager to catch up, she stood behind Daveny's shoulder and viewed Jeffrey's latest portfolio. One image in particular caught Kiara's attention. The picture was beautifully lit and framed. In it, Daveny and Collin held Jeffrey between them in a gesture both loving and protective. "You're so blessed. What a beautiful family."

"Tired, but blessed, yes." She sidled Kiara a look. "Which reminds me. Will you be seeing Ken in the next few days?"

"Not sure. Why?"

"Oh, nothing. No big deal."

Kiara gave her shoulder a nudge. "C'mon. What's up?"

"Well, there's prep material Collin wanted to deliver to him before the next Parish Council meeting. I'd love to keep close to home these days, at least until everyone is feeling better and I'm certain I've dodged the flu bullet. I only thought if you might be seeing him…"

"Stop being silly. I'd be happy to deliver it for you. I'll drop it by the church. No problem."

Oh, heavens, Kiara thought in a prompt back-pedal. *I leaped at that opportunity now didn't I?* Which was exactly why Daveny had floated the idea. Her knowing grin confirmed Kiara's assumption. "Are you sure?"

"Yeah. Really, it's no biggie." Acting casual, Kiara took possession of the large white envelope Daveny offered.

"Thanks, Kiara. I really appreciate it. Tell Ken I'll see him Sunday—good Lord willing."

14

Day one back on the job edged toward a close.

Ken sat across from Maggie Voorhees at a small conference table tucked into the far corner of his office. After straightening the pages of the most current edition of the budget and tucking them away inside a folder, Maggie leaned back in her chair. She struck Ken as being restless, tapping her pen on top of the legal pad upon which she had prioritized action items for the coming week.

Patiently he waited; he knew Maggie well enough to realize she'd express herself when she was ready.

"So, the word's getting out," she said at last.

Already starting to realign some financial allocations, Ken looked up from the spreadsheet he studied. "Hmm? Word?"

Maggie nodded, but chewed on the corner of her lip in a nervous habit of hers. It seemed she wanted very much to say something, but hesitated. Red flag number one lifted up and rippled. "Talk is going on about you. And Kiara."

Hello, red flag number two. Ken nearly sighed, but didn't. After all, gossip was a part of the human condition, and Woodland was far from exempt. "What about me and Kiara?"

"Well, the trip back was pretty illuminating, I have to say. Some of the kids from the youth group were talking in whispers during the trip home, and…"

The sentence trailed off, but Ken easily polished it off. Maggie and her husband had overheard. Amy, who had witnessed the kiss with Kiara, hadn't been able to resist the siren call of informing her friends about what had happened in the woods. The intent wasn't malicious or mean-spirited at all. Ken knew that without question. Still, Amy had figuratively spilled the beans about him and Kiara. From there, he felt sure a few friends had told a few more friends, until before long the eyes and ears of the Woodland Church community would rest upon their comings and goings—every look, touch, and communication.

Stemming from simple curiosity, the scrutiny would be harmless for the most part, but unnerving nonetheless.

Then, Maggie blew that piece of naïveté to bits. "Isn't she a little…I don't know…high-brow…for the kind of life you lead, Ken?"

"What?" Astounded by her unexpected and brazen comment, he could only stammer his way across the word.

"Look, don't get me wrong, I adore Kiara—she's been a God-send to Woodland, but she's hardly a staid, calming influence. And she's so different from Barb."

"Yes, she is, but that fact has no bearing on anything. That's not good or bad. A large part of what draws me to her is the fact that she's lively. She has passion and drive. She's spirited. She's also—and I can say this with one hundred percent conviction after spending an entire week on mission with her— completely devoted to her relationship with Woodland, and with God. What more would a person need?"

"Ken, I don't mean to offend. It's just that I can't see her settling for—" Maggie coughed quick and performed a fast edit of her words. "—settling *into* a life with a pastor. Honestly. Can you? I don't want her to hurt you, and I don't want her hurt either. It doesn't quite gel for me."

"Well fortunately, you're not the one it needs to *gel* for. Furthermore, this discussion of my life, and Kiara's, is now bordering on inappropriate."

Her eyes went wide. "Funny. I thought I was talking to a *friend* right now. I thought I was talking to someone who's been with me through good times and bad—and vice versa, for well over a decade now. I'm not talking to a pastor. I'm talking to the man I've known, who's been a friend to me, ever since he walked in the door. We've always had each other's backs."

He nodded. "True. But never once have we tried to tell one another what was right or wrong in our lives."

She regarded Ken in silence for a time, her lips a tight line. He could almost see the wheels turning— responses forming and vanishing. "Just be careful. Understandably, losing Barb put you in a spiral. In a completely different way, I worry that Kiara could do the very same thing."

In a ruffled, hot silence, they turned to leave the conference table. Ken's gaze traveled to the office doorway. That's when he heard Maggie draw a sharp breath, and he nearly dropped his paper-stuffed file folder.

Kiara stood framed in the threshold, an envelope in hand. Her expression was smooth, but her eyes were veiled. How much had she heard? Ken's chest felt constricted and his heart pounded.

"Ken, I have a delivery from Collin. Daveny gave it to me at work today. It's for the council meeting next week." She stepped inside as graceful as a movie star, gave him the envelope without missing a beat and even offered up a smile to Maggie. "How are you?"

"I'm good. Recovering, finally." Maggie's answer was friendly and warm, but she shuffled from foot to foot. All Ken wanted to do was fold Kiara into a tight hug. Other than slightly heightened skin, Kiara gave no indication whatsoever of having heard a word that had been exchanged.

Just looking at her, though, and knowing her the way he did, Ken didn't doubt she had heard the conversation. And if she hadn't heard all of it, she had heard more than enough to be upset—though in stalwart fashion, she hid that fact well. Ken realized he was probably one of the few who knew just how easily, and just how well, she could mask the hurt of being degraded.

"Returning to normal sleep patterns is a good thing, isn't it?" Kiara remarked with an almost too-bright tone. "Well, I'll see you both on Sunday. G'night, guys."

Turning away, her body language typically graceful and smooth, she left, but her pace was a bit quicker than Ken would have expected under normal circumstances.

"Maggie, I'll talk to you later."

He moved in haste and didn't stop until he caught up with Kiara. She had already made it to her car, and was currently wrestling with an un-giving door handle. He moved in fast behind her and slid his hands against hers until she went still. She didn't look at him.

He maneuvered her grasp away from the door handle and she froze in place. She squeezed her hands into fists.

"Come inside," he beckoned quietly. "Talk to me."

She did a good job of shrugging off his urging touch against her back, resuming her battle with a key fob that wouldn't unlock her door, and a door handle that refused to open. He felt like saying, *Kiara, sweetheart, take the hint.*

This time he took hold of both her hands and turned her fully away from the car. "Please come back inside."

"Don't, Ken. Not right now."

"Yes, now. Period. Come with me."

On the way in, they crossed paths with Maggie who was just leaving. Maggie issued a quick goodnight, and scurried to her car. Kiara sighed. "It sure didn't take long, now did it? I don't know why I feel angry at Maggie. Her heart's in the right place, even if her words stung. I have to give her snaps for being brave enough to say what everyone else is going to be thinking."

Heat boiled through his blood. "Don't do this Kiara. Don't get all wrapped up in other people. That's a pattern you need to break, isn't it?" She turned her head and glared at him. Ken pressed on, undeterred. "It's hard enough venturing into a new relationship under the best of circumstances, but…"

"But *what*?" Her barking retort, her blazing eyes left something inside him crumbling. Into those fissures and cracks came demons, lapping up his anxieties and doubts and fertilizing them deeply.

They finally reached the sanctuary of his office. Ken shut the door and turned, facing her eye to eye.

This was a matter they needed to resolve. Now.

"How much did you overhear?"

She pretended to ponder for a moment, tilting her head and pursing her lips. "I believe it started with something to the effect of me being a bit...what was the phrase? *High-brow* to ever settle for a life with a pastor."

With that, the worst-case scenario came to be. She had heard it all, a silent witness to someone knocking them down at a most fragile and vulnerable point in time.

He sighed heavily and sat on the front edge of his desk. He leaned forward, clasping his hands between his legs, inching as near to Kiara as he dared. She stood, stiff and apart from him, her arms folded protectively against her midsection.

He started to reach out, wanting to eliminate the distance between them, but she backed away a step. That riled his anger. "Kiara, do you think you're the only one who suffers from self-doubts here?"

"What do you mean by that? Are you lending credence to what Maggie had to say?"

Ken blew out a breath. After that came a pounding, redolent silence. "The point can be made that, that you and I...that elements of, of..."

"Out with it," she demanded. "Respect me enough to come clean. What's at the bottom of this, Ken? Tell me."

"OK." He paused, and looked at her steadily. "First of all, realize something important. Maggie wasn't criticizing *you*. She wasn't judging *you*. She was looking at a mix. A mix of your life with mine. I admit it. I've asked myself lately, what do I bring to you? How does my world enhance yours? My life is modest.

Simple. It's fulfilling to me, it's rewarding, and I treasure every moment of it, but I'm not meant to embrace the grand scale in ways that you have, in ways that you transformed yourself in order to find. How can I compete? How can I fulfill the part of your soul that longs for so much more than I can give?" This time he took hold of her hands and squeezed tight. "That's not a criticism, by the way. It's part of who you are. It's beautiful. *You're* beautiful. You're charming, you sparkle and you possess such vitality. But will we be *right*? Would you be happy? The only life I know is that of a pastor. A missionary. Is that your calling? Is it what's meant to be for you?"

By the end of Ken's speech, her eyes had filled, sparkling with tears. Her hands went limp and lifeless in his. Then, tears fell, and he felt powerless to do anything but go silent, and stare. Meanwhile, she watched him right back.

He had hurt her. Badly. A blade slid neat and deep against his heart. She swiped away the moisture, murmuring, "I understand. I get it." Her lips trembled. She firmed her jaw, but a pair of tears became a glimmering track against her fair, flawless skin. Kiara turned away by a fraction and pressed her fingertips against the bridge of her nose. "But I always thought actions spoke louder than words. I thought I had come so far, and shown you how much…"

At that point, her words ceased and she made a low, frustrated sound in her throat. When she looked into Ken's eyes, her pain transformed the blade cut into sharp, sizzling heat.

"What you just said," she whispered, "It confirms the worst fears I ever entertained about my feelings for you. And that rips my heart to pieces, Ken. I let myself believe. But I'll tell you what else," she continued, her voice now strong and steady despite the telling line of moisture shimmering on her cheeks. "I've grown. And I've changed." Ken moved to automatically cut in and agree with her. She sliced that action short with an abrupt motion of her hand and plowed ahead. "When we were in Pennsylvania, you told me you have faith in me. You told me you believe in me. Well do you, or don't you? You asked me to find out who I am. You urged me to become the best possible version of myself. Well that's what I've done. That's what I'm going to continue to do, no matter what. Not for you, not for me, but for the person I want to be before God. What you're saying right now is hurtful. It cuts away at that foundation I'm building, but I won't let it hurt me anymore. Maybe that's something else I needed to learn—that I have to fight for what I want, and who I am, and who I want to be. Well, don't ever get in the way of that again. I deserve better, and now I won't accept anything less." She straightened and looked at him with narrowed eyes. Strength of conviction rolled off her in waves, creating a God-made masterpiece, a formidable woman, inside and out. "Talk to me again once you've sorted that out."

Chin up, her eyes now blinked clear, Kiara spun, striding out of his office before he could even begin to recover from the staggering blow of hurt he had unwittingly inflicted—on both of them.

15

"Hey, Ken. These are for you, from Amy. She dropped them by the office the other day." The Parish Council meeting was about to begin. Maggie Voorhees approached in the posture of one who sought to make amends, with caution and penitence. Like a peace offering, she handed him an envelope full of photos.

"Thanks, Maggie." He capped the words with a warm smile, hoping to reestablish comfort. She had been an ace in the office, as usual, but since the episode with Kiara, she had avoided prolonged conversations, which was highly unusual for the two of them. He felt grateful for forward progress.

With Maggie, anyhow. Kiara remained a different, and difficult, matter all together.

He had a minute to spare before the meeting was called to order. Curious, he lifted the flap and inside found a neatly printed note from Amy:

Hi, Pastor Ken! I hope you like these. I think they came out pretty good! There are two sets—one for you, and one for Kiara. Can you please give them to her? You'll probably see her before I do. Thanks, and I'll see you in church! Amy

His lips quirked and his heart filled. It seemed Maggie wasn't the only one wanting to reaffirm friendship and care.

Members of the council took their seats. As people settled in, Ken shuffled through the pictures. A group shot taken on the last day rested on top, an instant source of bittersweet nostalgia. He missed…

Kiara.

He missed seeing her daily. He missed the passion and intensity they poured into the mission, and into discovering each other. Why did that realization leave him so conflicted? The love he felt for her was genuine, so why did the arguments he had made to her days ago still resound? Had he, without ever consciously meaning to, led her on? On one hand, was he *ready* for a deep-seated relationship? On the other, could he exist in happiness any longer without her?

He didn't think so. The more time that passed without her, the more his entire being seemed to ache, consumed by need and emptiness. Somehow, he had bungled and fallen. Somehow, he had refused delivery on a gift from God Himself. Kiara filled him. Ken couldn't escape that truth.

Still, there was a flip side he had to explore and resolve. Maggie had observed Kiara's vibrancy and enchanting charm. The statement was true, but guilt came into play whenever he considered the fact that while Barb's life had drifted away from him, Kiara's had swirled inexorably toward, pushing him into life and away from grief. Kiara inspired feelings he feared to face because even now, two years after Barb's death, entertaining the idea of a full and loving relationship with Kiara felt like a betrayal. Ken hadn't lied when he told Kiara he longed for much more time with Barb than they had been given. But his responses to Kiara—in body, heart and spirit—weren't a lie, either.

Despite the tumult, Kiara filled him with hope; her essence and life slid against his senses, enticed his soul to a place so beautiful it defied description.

Ken cleared his throat of a sudden tightness and kept thumbing through the images, continuing to drift away from reality. Now he studied a shot of Kiara and the kids, all in a row, securing landscape borders, then planting flowers and shrubs. Interior shots came after that. There was one of Ken perched on a ladder with a paint roller in hand, surrounded by members of the youth group. Then there was another of a crew of teens and contractors installing drywall and cabinetry.

The final two shots, however, commanded his total focus. First, a picture of him and Kiara. They wore large smiles, their arms around each other. Behind them stood the refurbished home of Casey Kidwell.

The last image featured the two of them on a wooden bench by the lake. Before them crackled a vibrant campfire. Kids encircled the dancing flames and dusk painted the photo in hues of rich blue. Kiara's legs were tucked beneath her, her body turned toward Ken's. In the photograph, he looked away from her, watching Tyler who could be seen strumming his beloved guitar.

What captured Ken about this moment in time was the way Kiara looked at him. Her eyes were unguarded, the dawn of a smile just beginning to curve her lips. Affection well beyond the superficial, and unseen by Ken at the time, telegraphed straight from the image to his heart.

A woman so beautiful, so full of magnetism, looked at him like that? Ken's world rolled over neatly then wobbled slowly back into place. He separated the two pictures, studying them for a few seconds longer before setting them on top of the pack. They were awesome.

"Ken? Ah—*Ken*..." Collin's summons broke

through Ken's fog-veiled mind. Ken snapped to attention and Collin waited for a moment, until he realized Ken was completely lost. "Are you ready to deliver the opening prayer?"

"Yes. Absolutely. I'm sorry for being distracted."

Ken tucked the photos beneath his agenda folder. The meeting moved forward from there and he paid much closer attention. Collin, however, kept tabs. He sent a couple covert glances Ken's way as Woodland's governing body hashed out church business.

Afterward Collin hung back while Ken exchanged good-byes and some final comments with those who departed. Curious about why Collin remained seated and made slow work of gathering paperwork, Ken bussed the table, depositing napkins and Styrofoam cups into a nearby trash can.

At last Collin stood. He took Ken by surprise when he asked, "You in the mood for a beer?"

Ken stopped his cleaning duties to look at him. "I could be talked into it—so long as I don't end up getting in trouble with Daveny."

Collin grinned. "I sent her a text right after we adjourned. Jeffrey's sound asleep so I'm in the clear for an hour or so. Does Grissom's Pub sound good?"

Ken nodded. "Done. I didn't get dinner. I'm starving."

࿊

A Wednesday edition of Sports Center played in the background. Ken followed Collin to a table toward the rear of Grissom's where they could talk at reasonable decibels yet at the same time monitor the latest news from the NFL. Ken ordered the house special—burger, fries and a brew. Collin followed suit.

"Those were some great pictures," Collin commented right off the bat. "Especially the ones of you and Kiara at the end. Tell me about the trip."

Uh-oh. I'm in for it. Disconnected from his surroundings at the start of the Parish Council meeting, Ken hadn't realized until now just how close Collin had been watching.

"It was great," he said and cut it off right there. He focused on the plasma screen above them. The smack of pool balls added occasional punctuation to the atmosphere.

"If you think you're getting off that easy, think again, pal."

Their waitress delivered a pair of longnecks, giving Ken just enough time to put up a wall of defense. "Is this an inquisition, or are we going to enjoy having a beer?" Ken tempered the words with a grin then took a swallow of his brew.

Collin followed suit as he pretended to think about that question for a second. "I vote for both." He hit Ken with a probing look. "It's payback time."

Ken couldn't help laughing. Payback indeed.

"You remember my anger at God. You helped me destroy that wall I had around my heart after Lance was killed. You lost your wife. I lost my oldest brother. When I clawed my way back, it was Daveny, and you, who threw me lifelines. You helped me find my way back to faith, to Christ."

Ken had a part to play in that redemptive process, sure, but God worked the miracle. God's faithfulness astounded Ken anew each time he recognized the active, caring role Collin now assumed with his faith and Woodland. For a number of years, until he met

Daveny, Collin had full-out rebuked God. Now he not only attended church, he took on an active role as a newly elected Parish Council member.

In the process of Collin's struggle, Ken had welcomed him back to church, and even challenged him to leave behind emptiness so he could embrace a new point of view with regard to his spirit-life and his relationship with God. It seemed Collin had learned his lessons well.

Collin continued, echoing Ken's thought pattern. "You helped me find my footing. Let me return the favor."

To stall, he took another pull on his beer. Instinct left Ken wanting to step neatly to the side, shrug off what he felt. He didn't want to bring people into his personal turmoil. Dealing with Barb's illness had made him somewhat of a pro at that maneuver. Tonight, however, he shunted that instinct and instead moved toward Collin's offer of friendship.

"OK. I'll cut to the chase for you. She's fantastic, obviously. But I could never keep her interested, Collin. Mine isn't the kind of life she's been looking for. My life is simple. It's about church guidance, serving God, and being present to the members of my parish. It's about church events and budgetary red ink. Meanwhile, Kiara receives offers to jet away to Europe."

"Which she turned down, remember."

Ken shrugged. "Point taken. True. But the fact remains, her life features excitement and adventure. An excitement and adventure she craves."

"Act for one hot second like that isn't exactly what draws you to her."

Hmmm. So Collin wanted to play hardball. Ken

battled right back. "It is. I won't deny it, but therein lies the rub. She's all about embracing new experiences with the people she draws into her life with nothing more than that smile of hers and the easy, attractive way she just *is*. I'm nobody's sophisticate. I'm not electric like she is."

"Oh yes you are," Collin said definitively. "Every time you step up to proclaim God's word, or deliver a sermon, you capture people. It's all in a matter of what you're passionate *about*. It's all in the matter of what God calls you to *do*. You found your calling and embraced it from the get-go. You settled in nicely with Barb. Then, a seismic change occurred. You've had to reevaluate your entire life.

"Now go the other way. Take a good look at Kiara. At her spirit. What does it tell you? Ken, she's doing exactly the same thing you are! She's looking for her calling. She's stepping away from the life she thought she wanted, with all of its temptations and allure, and she's looking for something Godly. Something to fill her soul. She's finding God, and in the process, she's finding *you*. Take the hint." Ken stared, swept into Collin's words and struck silent.

"What I'm saying is, be ready for the chance God's giving you to be a partner to a woman who wants, and *needs*, someone just like *you*. Not to satisfy who she *was*, but who she's *becoming*."

Ken ran his thumb along the cold, moist surface of the bottle he held. "You make it sound so easy."

"It's not."

Ken appreciated that comment and gave Collin a quick glance. "I suppose it's easy for some people to write off the confusion I feel, or just not understand it. Get over it, some may say. Barb's gone. Move on."

Collin gaped. "I'd personally deal with anyone who was that cold about the relationship you had with Barb." He gave Ken a sheepish look. "Forgive the impulse toward violence."

Ken laughed, fingering the cocktail napkin beneath his beer. "Forgiven. Thing is? I can't seem to reconcile myself to let go. On one level, I'm giving over to Kiara. It's like I can't even *help* it. On another, I *want* to hold back. I feel guilty, and definitely afraid. I want to be everything to her, and I know I can't be."

"Let me ask you something."

"Yeah?"

"Is guilt and fear what you were thinking about when you looked at those pictures?"

Ken nodded then sheepishly came clean. "And more."

"I figured out the *and more* part solo." He gave Ken a wry grin, and then continued. "Look, seriously, I'm not belittling what you've said. I'm only asking so you can think about things. What is it about the situation with Kiara that's giving you so much guilt? Is there something about her, or you, that makes you feel this way? As Barb's illness progressed, Kiara's presence in your life sharpened focus. There's no shame in that."

"Not from where I sit," Ken murmured.

Their food arrived, steaming and fragrant, along with a second round of beers. They gave thanks and dug in.

"You know? Really? All I ever wanted was to live my life in guidance of Woodland, happily married to a wonderful woman—a woman I treasure and cherish. Someone to create a family with."

"That's still a possibility. In fact, it would seem to be a very *good* possibility."

"Maybe, Collin, but...but I just can't—dive in to Kiara."

"You're forgetting something." Collin tipped back his beer then downed a trio of fries. "I watched you tonight. Your face tells me the truth that your words won't. I'd say the dive you're talking about already happened; you just need to face it."

Ken stared. Collin's verdict left him no escape hatch. Ken couldn't deny the comment, but he couldn't move forward yet, either. "Know what I feel like?"

"What?"

"A teenager. A teenager with a raging crush. I feel like the high-school geek who's fallen hard for the homecoming queen."

Collin feasted on his burger, and so did Ken.

"You know," Collin said at length, "Kiara would absolutely, without a question or a doubt, *hate* that analogy."

"I know. I'd never say anything like that to her directly, but I can't help how I feel—"

Collin cut him off. "Back up a sec. I'm lost. When exactly did you become the *geek* in this story?"

Ken laughed. "OK, OK. I'm not a geek, but in so many ways it's a similar situation." He turned, squaring off directly with his friend. "Let me clarify the point I'm trying to make—and I can absolutely, without a question or a doubt guarantee that Kiara would agree with what I'm about to say."

Collin smirked at Ken's parroting job, but he listened.

"Kiara's told me herself that she sees me as something up here." Ken held his hand shoulder high. "I'm a pastor, which means—"

"Oh, man, which means you definitely shouldn't

be at a local watering hole tossing back a couple brews with a parish member. Cripe. Gimme that beer right now before you lose your preaching license or something "

"Collin, you're a jerk. As I was saying, I'm up here, while the rest of mere mortal humanity lies somewhere down here." His hand lowered to almost brush the wood tabletop. "I'm different. Set apart. So you see, while I may not be a geek, it's the same difference." He pointed at Collin. "And the results are just the same, too. Know what I mean?"

"Well, maybe that's because you met and married Barb before you became a full-blown church leader. A comfort zone had already been established, right?"

"Yeah."

"Could that be part of what's upsetting the balance for you and Kiara? That the *comfort zone* just isn't there for Kiara? Yet?"

"Yet?"

"*Yet.* Because it seems to me that during the mission trip, you came down from the mountain a bit, and Kiara found her way upward. Judging by the sapped-out look on your face when you thumbed through those pictures, progress was made. And progress is progress. In fact, I'll bet she's *counting* on you. So don't let her down, and don't you dare give up." Collin sent a direct, penetrating look in Ken's direction. "You gonna give up?"

Collin's words struck him like a bell being chimed. Ken *had* let her down. He had told her not to worry. He had told her they would make it through. But then he had performed an abrupt and shattering back pedal. Out of fear.

Out of a lack of faith.

Lights in Ken's heart clicked on, illuminating a few of his more unsettling errors in judgment. He gave Collin the most honest, bare-bones answer he could. "I can't give up. To do that would be impossible."

Collin stretched back and spread his hands wide seeming to claim victory. Before digging in to his food again, he lifted his beer bottle and *thunked* it against Ken's. They swallowed a tandem swig then Collin grinned at him, "Then go get her—and my work here is finished."

Ken made plans. He'd talk to her after church this weekend. He'd take her home and make her breakfast after services. They'd talk—really talk—about a future. Together.

The idea left Ken smiling, and Collin just looked at him with a knowing smirk. Ken snapped to proper attention and they continued their meal companionably before Collin remarked, "So—now to the stuff that's *really* important."

Ken chuckled, weights unbuckling from his heart, allowing it to rise. "Which is?"

After wiping his mouth on a napkin, Collin munched on a French fry and looked up at the television screen, promptly losing himself in Sports Center. "Do you think the Lions are *ever* gonna climb out of the NFL cellar?"

16

Kiara immersed herself deep within the landscape design for a law firm in Bloomfield Hills. Thus settled, she only vaguely registered the tinkling alert of an incoming text message to her cell phone. Next came a more persistent vibration that sent the device skittering across the surface of her desk until it bumped and stalled against an open folder of renderings and lay-out plans.

Concentration shattered, her thoughts turned instantly to Ken. She fought the urge to growl. Growling wouldn't do when she wore her professional demeanor—but plenty times of late she growled, stammered her way through ineffective mutterings, unanswered prayers, shivers of loneliness, and a pervasive, overriding need that rolled through her over and over and over again. Especially in the night. Especially when her body and mind sought refuge, rest and peace from loving him so much. The silence permeated her world. Obviously, Ken had written off their relationship as mutually unsuitable.

Days had passed since she stumbled upon the exchange between Ken and Maggie, and the lack of communication left her roiling. What was Ken thinking? Going through? Granted, she had turned away, but by the same token, Ken hadn't reached out either. That spoke volumes.

A headache bloomed. Not an uncommon development these days. She worked her fingertips fruitlessly against a tight knot of tension that ran a circuit from her neck to her shoulders straight on down to her back. With stubbornness of will, she refused delivery and acknowledgement of her pain—again— and forced Ken Lucerne to a locked chamber of her heart.

Once again, she hunkered down with layout plans for the sweeping roll of land upon which rested the stately, Colonial designed headquarters of Stuart and Littleson, Attorneys at Law. She lost herself in work, mapped out bush and tree possibilities. She plotted the perfect display and color scheme of annuals, perennials, and accents like ultra-fine gravel in glimmering shades of pearl, or perhaps a more dramatic red stone border frame...

She pushed and pushed, relentless and hyper focused. She wanted—she needed—anything that would take her thoughts, and heart, far from an image that kept crowding her brain. The image came to her regardless. Spirit enticing warmth, flowing straight out from clear brown eyes, a wide smile framed by soft, full lips—lips she could now taste and feel...a rich, deep voice, a commanding, compelling personality.

Kiara straightened in her chair. She pinched the bridge of her nose and rolled her shoulders, finally picking up the cell phone, which, though silent, now flashed a tiny red attention light. Apparently, she was such a mess she now needed a distraction from distraction. She needed to keep herself from holding on so tightly to someone who, by virtue of their final words and a building silence, wanted nothing more to do with her.

She opened the text message, from a girlfriend, Anne Marie, who tended to coordinate group gatherings.

220 Morrill
Sunday @ 10 am
Brunch w/the gang
Bacon, eggs n gossip
U in?

The invite left her with mixed emotions. Once-upon-a-Kiara would have been filled with the happy expectation of a high-end meal with friends. But she was starting to wonder. Were these really her friends? Did they have her heart, and did she have theirs? Were they all simply convenient counterparts, possessing similar goals and life points, staving off an ever-present void by pushing one another with the goal of professional and material success?

Quite frankly, her time with Ken left Kiara questioning everything. Pastor Ken Lucerne had opened her heart and filled it up with God's promise and grace, and the power of love. For a time, she had actually tasted fulfillment, experienced a sense of spiritual growth that made her happier than anything else she could remember.

She missed him so much she literally ached— especially in those moments when she found herself most alone, when vulnerability climbed to its highest peak—when dreams and memories turned into a tantalizing swirl.

Now only emptiness remained.

Pain twisted its way through a deep, heretofore impenetrable area of Kiara's spirit. She reviewed the invitation to 220—a favorite restaurant of hers in downtown Birmingham. Ten o'clock in the morning on a Sunday. That would mean missing church.

And for some odd reason, that realization caused her worst, most painful memory to descend...her final words to Ken.

"You told me you have faith in me. That you believe in me. Well do you, or don't you? You asked me to find out who I am. You urged me to become the best possible version of myself. Well that's what I've done. That's what I'm going to continue to do, no matter what. Not for you, not for me, but for the person I want to be before God."

Noble? Sure. Meant it whole-heartedly? At the time, absolutely. But now Kiara felt weak. Her strength waned, siphoned pint by pint and replaced by overwhelming pain and need. Did anything really make a difference? And honestly—would missing a Sunday service truly matter? She needed a taste of her old life—of the old Kiara.

Pain continued to grow, blooming into a debilitating burn. She went tense, jiggling her crossed leg nervously. She clenched the cell phone tight and started to rapid-fire click the keys. With a resolute push of the "send" button, she returned a simple, three word reply:

Count me in.

∫∫

"We're here today," Anna Marie began, "to toast the end of an era. To mourn the death of manslayer supreme, Kiara Jordan, who is a newly sanctified Holy Roller and mission worker. So, tell us about the trip."

Anna Marie lifted her flute of orange juice and the half-dozen people gathered at their table followed suit. Kiara's beverage remained untouched. She couldn't bring herself to join in the chortles. The way Anna Marie emphasized the words *Holy Roller* rankled her nerves something fierce.

Yep—this brunch date was one colossal mistake.

Sharing a meal at 220 Merrill with the gang didn't sit well with her today. Elements of this get together rubbed her in places which were already raw and aggravated. Well, she supposed, this kind of newness, this revised perception, shouldn't be shocking. She had changed a great deal recently.

So Kiara glowered at Anna Marie, delivering a tight, unfeeling grin. "Thanks so much for the eulogy, Anna Marie. Really. That's so nice."

The group laughed and teased as Kiara rolled her eyes and finally sipped her drink. But she didn't chink glasses with everyone else. At one time, perhaps the guffaws and bawdy comments that followed her comment would have seemed harmless—nothing more than good-natured fun and one-upmanship.

Not anymore.

Reaching beneath the surface of this group revealed much more. The mention of God's power and mission taken out of proper context hit Kiara first; then the lack of sensitivity hit her heart. The joking session left her aching instead of laughing. No one asked about the truth of her mission trip, or its impact on her heart. Truthfully, they didn't care. That was fair enough. What she disliked was the fact that she was being torn down and mocked based on conviction of belief.

Kiara had slipped into her former role for this gathering. It was comfortable to her right now. Familiar. She wore a Michael Kors cashmere twin set of delicate pink, and the cardigan presently rested on the chair behind her. A slim cut, royal blue skirt of silk was paired with leg flattering high-heeled pumps crafted by Ferragamo. The hair and makeup were perfect, but the needs of her soul beat relentlessly against her heart, refusing to be still, or quiet, any longer.

She glanced at the slim gold bangle watch on her wrist. It was almost eleven. Right about now, services at Woodland would be winding down. Ken would be doing everything in his power to wrap the church in God's embrace—though preaching and presence.

She bit her lips together to ward off the pain, the ache of longing. Her counterparts didn't even notice the fact that she'd retreated, inch by inch, during the course of the meal. They were so wrapped up in their own worlds they didn't focus outward. Meanwhile, Kiara picked at her mandarin salad and did her best to simply endure.

Conversation ebbed and flowed while she faded into the background and discreetly checked her watch again. She could make a getaway soon. A beautiful Sunday called, and she longed to spend it in a more productive, contented way.

If only, if only, if only…

"Hey, Kiara."

The summons came from behind and she braced against the sound of a deep, perfectly modulated voice. Kiara stifled a cringe, but it took tremendous effort. Andrew. Perfect. Her day glided into an even steeper downward angle. She wanted to scream she felt so displaced and sad. Now, on top of it all, *Drew*. She did the best and only thing she could. She surrendered herself for a few precious seconds, and prayed:

Lord Jesus, please help me. I miss Ken so much. I miss the constancy of our connection during the mission trip. I miss the love we shared in furthering Your kingdom, and discovering one another. Lord, please help us and guide us according to Your will. I promise to try to trust You even more. I can't fight any longer. Forgive me for even trying. I'm tired and I feel broken. Ease this ache, this longing that keeps tearing away at my spirit.

Polite behavior dictated she turn and greet Drew, so that's what she did, but all Kiara really wanted to do was leave. She wanted Ken.

"Hi, Drew. How are you?"

"Good." He quickly scanned the faces of the people at the table. "Ah, if you have a few minutes, I'd like to talk to you."

Kiara's mind raced through the scenario, and within it, she sensed an escape hatch. She could dismiss herself from the table, spend a moment or two with Drew, then leave. The promise of an imminent exit from 220 beckoned to her like beautiful music.

So after a quick goodbye, a couple of air kisses to her girlfriends and empty-sounding promises of outings to come, Kiara shouldered her purse. She hitched her sweater from the chair and followed Drew to a couple of empty stools at the nearby bar where they settled.

"Want a drink or anything?"

"No thanks, I'm good."

Drew just nodded. Kiara waited, and resisted the urge to check her watch for what had to be the dozenth time.

"Welcome back," he offered.

Drew's hesitance softened Kiara's heart, and she smiled at him. "Thanks. It's good to be home, but I'll be honest. I miss the Kidwells already. I love what we were able to accomplish for them. It was the best—we helped fixed a roof, built a bedroom addition, landsca—"

Drew wasn't really listening. His attention was focused elsewhere. As her words trailed off, he reached out to touch Kiara's wrist. Brows knit, he studied the simple and precious bracelet that had not left her possession since Amber settled it into place.

"What's this?" he asked.

His interruption struck her as rude, and his tone felt accusing. In counterpoint, she kept her reply smooth. "A gift from the family we helped out. It was made for me by one of the kids."

Andrew shrugged, and made a noncommittal sound. Meanwhile Kiara touched the beads, absorbing the memory of faith and love, the gratitude built in to each one. Her focus rested on the piece as a memory slid against her like satin.

"Thank you—for being the face of Christ to these people, Kiara, in word and in deed. Your commitment has made a huge difference in their lives."

Ken's words sang through her mind, a source of reassurance. In phantom, she felt his kiss, his tender touch. Most of all, though, his powerful example lent her fledgling spirit some much-needed strength of resolve, as well as the assurance of God's unconditional love.

Andrew interrupted those thoughts. "You know? I have to say, I just don't get it. Frankly, I'm shocked that someone as worldly as you would get pulled in by a program like that. I mean, they're fine enough I suppose, but at the end of the day—"

"They're fine enough? Someone as worldly as me? Gee. Thanks for the show of support, Drew. This was, and is, important to me."

His eyes widened with surprise. "OK. I get it."

She sighed inwardly, saying, "I wish you did. What about the equation of me helping people and committing myself to God, doesn't make sense, Drew?"

For a moment, he just looked uncomfortable. He shrugged again, and astonishment flooded her. To think, just a short time ago she had been tempted to abandon her core dreams and beliefs in favor of a sensual odyssey with this man. Paris had called, as had the fleeting promise, and arms, of a successful, sexy man who, at his center, remained woefully empty.

It occurred to Kiara that chasing a placebo to loneliness might very well have been her undoing. Self-doubt may have cost her one of the most precious relationships God could provide.

Images skimmed and weaved through her mind, then clicked into focus like a high-res digital photo display: Amy and Tyler's playful sparring, Ken leading a campfire bonding session, the simple and breathtaking beauty of a country lake, its surrounding woods and the stars sparkling above, a grateful, jubilant family.

But it was Ken's image that repeated most often. The most powerful recollection was not of his pastoral uniform—the crisp black suit and white collar—nor his formal vestments. Instead, she recalled him decked out in an old WSU sweatshirt speckled by a trace of grease. Her heart held fast to the way he kept an ancient van in shape because it ran great, shuttled batches of kids efficiently, and remained reliable and performance-ready by virtue of his caring hand and commitment.

Even in loneliness and longing, Kiara treasured the time she had spent working side by side with him, helping a destitute family struggling to overcome life's harshest blows. Her heart swelled, filled by a love deeper, richer and more intoxicating than any emotion she had ever known.

At last, Drew continued. "You asked why this doesn't make sense to me. You want my answer? Seriously?"

"Yes."

"Good, because in all honesty it's the reason why I want to talk to you."

Kiara waited. Meanwhile, Drew shifted in his seat. His disquiet seemed to grow. "I guess I'm more than a little surprised."

"At?"

"At *you*." He faced her fully now, and the look on his face made her bristle. There was dark challenge in his eyes. Big-time skepticism. "I have to admit, it surprises me that the modern-thinking, enlightened woman I know and wanted to get to know even better, has turned into a Jesus freak all because her pastor is some kind of an idealistic do-gooder."

How Kiara kept from gasping aloud would remain a forever mystery, attributable only to years of well-practiced control and emotional shielding. She blinked a few times. She leaned back and away from the close proximity of their shared space at the bar. Her voice, however, she regulated to low and even. "Ken Lucerne isn't a do-gooder. He lends a helping hand to those in need. Yes, that's idealistic. But my question to you is: when did that become something negative?"

"Maybe it's a jealousy factor," he retorted hotly. "Maybe I'm being negative because all you've been doing lately is singing his praises. If I didn't know any better, I'd think you were going all warm and cozy for your *religion* and a man of the *cloth* who's transforming you into something you're really *not*.. You—one of the most cosmopolitan people I know. I mean, Jes—"

"Stop it right there. And while we're at it, stop thinking you know me well enough to make any kind of informed judgments about my life."

"You mean to tell me you intend to waste that beauty," he gestured at her expansively, "that body," he gestured again. "And that sex appeal of yours? Get serious, Kiara!" With that, he sank against the edge of the bar and just stared.

Each word he spoke socked into her stomach like a fist, robbing her of precious air. She looked at him for an open-mouthed second and Andrew continued hotly. "Oh, come on! Are you surprised I feel this way? You're too intelligent and too vibrant a woman to waste time on the moral opiate of religion. That's not what life's about."

This time her breath caught. "Wow," she whispered. She shook her head, feeling hot and dizzy. "Just…wow." Kiara's breaking point came and went. "Let me make something clear to you, Drew. In my world, the sacrifice and love of my Lord and Savior isn't a moral opiate; it's the entire universe." She stood abruptly and hoisted her purse from the next seat. She yanked her sweater from its spot on the bar ledge and balled it in her fist. *To heck with cashmere.* "All I'm going to add is this: If being a *Jesus Freak* kept me from making the mistake of taking a hedonistic voyage with you to Europe, and kept me from a relationship that would have ended in emptiness and disaster, then I say more power to Him."

Kiara spun away; Andrew grabbed her hand. She jerked free of his touch, but stayed put while he said, "This kind of overreaction is *exactly* what I'm talking about. Sit down and stop acting so offended!"

She'd thought she couldn't be any more shocked. She was woefully wrong. "You ridicule my beliefs, mock a part of my life that's increasingly important to me, a part of my life I'm exploring, and growing into, yet you tell me to not act offended? Well here's a clue, Drew, I'm not *acting*."

His gaze darted left and right, no doubt checking for eavesdroppers and the attention of nearby patrons. "Would you *lighten up?* Seriously, do you see yourself as being that, I don't know, holy? Or righteous?" His tone made it sound like the terms *holy* and *righteous* were a bad thing. Thank God she had learned differently.

There was no need for more. Kiara shook her head, giving him a long, last look. "Goodbye, Drew."

Without another word, she left the restaurant. Her eyes stung, yet remained miraculously dry. She gasped a bit, struggling to still herself and just breathe as she strode to the nearby public lot where she had parked her car. She slid behind the wheel and started to drive. Tears built, periodically blurring her vision. Once they fell, Kiara dashed them away with a careless swipe; anger burbled through her bloodstream until she thought she would overflow with a blend of sadness and rage.

Not fully realizing her intent, not even aware of the direction she took, Kiara pulled into the parking lot at Woodland and stopped. There she sat in the car, resting her head on the steering wheel, finally letting the sobs overwhelm.

Nobody would understand her now. No one would recognize the impact of God's presence, or the turning of her heart toward service and faith rather than self-centered pursuits. But that was OK.

Because God does. Because, no matter what comes to be between the two of us, Ken does, too.

Right now, she wanted Woodland's sanctuary. She wanted Ken's presence, his tenderness, so desperately. At the same time, she heard the echo of Andrew's every word. The conversation brought her worst fears and self-doubts into a sharp and unforgiving focus. She wasn't worthy. She didn't deserve a man like Ken. Her life, to the point of meeting him, had been too vivid a compilation of unsuccessful relationships and selfish pursuits, the pain of which she masked with empty moments in dimly lit clubs and bars, competitive professional pursuits. The resulting circle of friends, save a few, weren't truly friends, for they didn't know her in the least. Hers was a quest for fulfillment. Yet the closer she came to authentic contentment, the more those around her watched in confusion.

Everyone except Ken. He thoroughly understood her evolution as a Christian; he encouraged her attempts and saw past her failures at faith building. Furthermore, in his hands rested the unquestioned key to her heart and happiness.

Dear Jesus, she prayed in silence, *please help me. I'm trying. I want to be worthy of You. I want to be worthy of a man who carries Your word and mission and truth into the world. I feel inadequate, and unfit to travel the pathway You're opening up in my heart, yet it answers every longing I have. I want to serve You, and I want to fulfill that role at Ken's side. Is that Your will? Is that Your plan? I just don't know. I'm not sure of anything anymore. I leave everything to You in surrender and trust. I want to give more of myself to You, Lord. Please give me the chance. Please help me."*

In the calm, pervasive stillness that filled the car,

Kiara fought to regain control. She grabbed a couple tissues from the storage compartment next to her seat. She dabbed her eyes, and cleared her runny nose. Steadying her trembles, she exited the car, considering a plan. She'd go inside and pray. She'd rest for a time inside the church.

That's when she surveyed the grounds of Woodland…

And there he was.

17

Ken walked the perimeter of the pond, tossing bread bits to the newest members of Woodland's family—a flock of Canadian geese. Kiara's heart performed a somersault, expanding with an emotion so powerful, so perfect it could only be captured in one small word. Love.

So this is what it felt like to leave behind a world full of haze and smoggy pollution to come upon fresh air, warmth and a tender, perfect light.

Overwhelmed once more, tears filled her eyes. She didn't even care. Need spurred her forward. She left the car behind and literally ran to him.

When he heard her footfalls, he turned, an expression of curiosity transforming immediately to concern when he saw her face. He didn't speak, and either did Kiara. She didn't want to talk. She wanted…she wanted…

At that exact moment, he opened his arms.

Kiara tumbled into his embrace and Ken held her steady and sure. He rubbed her back, and silently squeezed her tight.

Home. Her soul came to sureness and rest. *This is home.*

A sigh passed through her body, exiting on a soft release of air as she tried to wipe away tears. Ken still wore his pastoral uniform—the black slacks and shirt—the white collar and black suit coat. Her tears fell and she tried to pull away so she wouldn't make a mess of him, but he held her fast. Kiara rejoiced. Laying her head on his shoulder, she snuggled close and slid her fingertips beneath the lapel of his jacket, breathing in the sandalwood scent of him. "I'm blubbering all over you."

"It's OK. I missed you at services today. Very much. It was like a piece of me went missing."

Urgency coated his words. She knew the feeling well, so she opened herself and responded from the heart. "I'm so sorry for not being here. You have no idea what a mistake I made. But I learned something important today, if that's any consolation."

Ken swayed slightly, taking her with him on a subtle dance. "What's that?"

"It seems God can teach me a lesson whether I attended church or not." She leaned back, wanting to look into his eyes. She absolutely loved those sparkling, gentle eyes. "You're still dressed for work," she observed lamely. "Am I interrupting?"

He visually puzzled while studying her face. "Not at all. I'm headed to St. John's Hospital in a couple hours. I found out Pat Dunleavy is having an emergency heart cath procedure, so I want to visit him."

Typical. Did he have any clue at all what a miracle he was? Probably not. Meanwhile his warm, calloused fingertips slid against her cheek. He looked into her eyes, waiting on explanations. Kiara felt her eyes fill again, whether from gratitude for his presence or gratitude for peace and joy, she couldn't quite tell anymore. Cushioned within the haven of Ken's arms, she didn't even care.

"Come here, angel." He led her to a metal bench positioned at the edge of a pathway that cut through the lush grounds of the church. There they sat. Before them rolled a deep green carpet of grass that was pleasingly damp and dewy smelling. A few hearty, last-of-summer blooms colored the scene. Old trees with thick trunks held leaves bursting with fiery color. The pond and its geese, the arch of Parishoner's Bridge spanning its width, formed a lovely scene.

Ken fingered back the fall of her hair and slid it over her shoulder. He settled his arm along the curved back of the bench, opening himself, encouraging her close. She tucked in gratefully at his side.

"Can you tell me what happened?" he asked.

This wasn't a pastor asking a church member. This was man to woman. The difference was distinct, and bone melting. *Lord,* she beseeched, *please, please let there be love here. Deep, holy, abiding love…*

The instant his arm slid against her shoulder, the moment he drew her into the warm, solid wall of his body, Kiara wanted nothing but to dissolve into the respite he offered.

"Just for now, can explanations wait? Can I please just rest here? With you? It's all I want."

"Take all the time you need."

Kiara tucked her head into the crook of his shoulder and closed her eyes, doing just as she wished, and dreamed. She allowed herself to melt away and go absolutely calm, thinking: *If I could only have this for a lifetime…*

"Why is it I get so emotional around you?" she asked. "Why do all my emotions rise to the surface and spill over, whenever I'm with you?"

"Because you're safe. I promise that. I'll try not to

hurt you, or ever judge."

Kiara dipped her head, wiping her eyes with fingertips that were already moist. On cue, Ken handed her a handkerchief. Accepting the offering, she gave him a watery laugh. "I still have the one you gave me at Jeffrey's baptism, plus the one from Pennsylvania. My collection seems to be growing. I should get them back to you, but I keep forgetting."

Ken leaned in and dotted her nose with a lingering kiss. "Don't worry about that." He paused for a beat. "What happened, Kiara?"

It was time. It was time for the ultimate heart gambit—with God guiding the way. In His hands, no matter what the outcome, she knew without question she'd find a way to goodness, and grace. Such was her newfound faith.

So, Kiara took a deep breath. She looked out, at the waterline of Lake Saint Clair across the horizon, at the fiery tree leaves that heralded autumn in Michigan. Sunlight danced in and out of large, gray puffs of pure white clouds, painting the world around them in vivid, tantalizing colors.

"I think I started to answer a few questions today."

"About?"

She couldn't quite bring herself to say the words *Is my love for you what brings me to God, or is my love for God sufficient enough?* Instead, she replied, "Is my faith in God strong? Is it focused where it should be? I've discovered the answer is yes. To both."

Tired and spent, she luxuriated in the sensation of resting against him, though she finally detailed the episode that had taken place at 220 Merrill just a short time ago. Patient and steady, he watched after her, held her close, and listened.

"My friends refuse to see me in the framework of a Christian spirit; especially Drew. He couldn't see me living up to Christian principles. He said I was too enlightened and too intelligent to be drawn in by something as intangible as religion and faith. Ken, I got so mad at him, and I felt so hurt. It raised insecurities I have about my relationship with God. Stuff I need to really work on."

"Like what? What's holding you back?"

Not being good enough for the man I love so dearly.

That truth stalled in her throat. "I just...I can't quite bring myself to believe I'm worthwhile. Am I qualified to be a part of His mission?" *With you...?*

Yet again, that addenda item remained frozen inside her.

Ken quirked a finger beneath Kiara's chin and directed her gaze up to his. "Kiara, you answered that question as well. Take a close look at the past two months. Review what you intend to do from this point on, then answer that question for me. Right now. Honestly. From the gut. I want to hear you say it. *Are you qualified?*"

She could literally feel herself drift into his warmth. And he was right—despite everything between them, and despite everything rocking her world—she felt safe enough, and confident enough, to say, "Yes. Yes, I am."

Ken smiled and her heart took flight.

"Good answer," he said, stroking her cheek, causing her eyes to flutter closed on a flood of contentment. "You're human. Kiara. You'll succeed. You'll fail. The only guarantee is an imperfect trying, and that God loves each and every effort we make. Don't feel doubt because of someone else's misperceptions. Don't give other people that kind of power. That kind of thinking has been a weight on your shoulders for far too long."

"I know." She watched, enrapt, as the stroke of his hand against her neck, and shoulders, emphasized his point. Quietly, she continued. "He made me so angry. I left him feeling shocked at how angry and hurt I felt about the way he attacked people who believe in God, people who have faith."

"But you stood up to him. When you turned the tables on him, you did so by standing on your own two feet, and by relying on your own belief system rather than someone else's influence. I'd call that God inspired."

Brightness took root, expelling all else, warming her through. "Exactly. Dang but you're good, *Pastor* Ken."

"*Ken*," he corrected with a grin and a sparkle in his eyes that she loved. She wanted to just sink into him, to stay in this moment, this connectedness, forever. "In the end, no matter who, no matter what, no single person is ever going to fulfill you. At some point, we're all going to fail one another. We're going to fall short, no matter how good our intentions." He paused. "Even me."

That opened the doorway to all that lay between them—compatibility, mutual faith and trust. Love.

Kiara decided it was time to move forward, saying, "I was stubborn, and it was wrong of me to walk away from you the way I did."

"You were justified, because you were hurt. But please know, I never meant to—"

She silenced him by reaching up to stroke his lips closed. "That doesn't even need to be said," she whispered. "I know that without being told, Ken. It just...it *hit* me. Everything seemed to pile up on me, and open up old sores. My issue. Not yours. I know you were defending me—"

"Us," he clarified.

Us. The simple, two letter word slipped through her like a sweet, tempting breeze.

Ken continued. "But I blew it afterwards by showing I didn't have the kind of faith I urge everyone else to hold on to. I was going to talk with you after services today, and when you didn't show up, I honestly felt something inside me crumble. I wanted to take you home, make you breakfast, and at least *try* to explain myself. All I could think about the past couple days was having the chance to just be together outside of everything, and everyone, but each other."

Meanwhile she had suffered through that horrendous brunch. Kiara sighed out loud, sad for the emptiness they had both endured, but so very eager to make up for lost time, to build goodness anew. She sifted her fingertips through his hair and the subtle earth spice aroma of his shampoo was released. The scent tickled her nose, most intriguing...

"We need this, Kiara."

The tenor of his voice was promising, deep and rich. The power behind that statement filled her with delicious tingles. Just as quickly as it had been born, that biting ache of need she carried died in the arms of hope, and joy.

"But you have to go to the hospital."

Ken slid his fingers against hers, linking their hands together. "Not for a while yet. Will you come home with me?"

She nodded. He drew Kiara to her feet, and she

felt so light she wondered if she couldn't actually float away on the wind. Ironically, a punctuating breeze drifted against them, lifting her hair, causing a few strands to dance across her face. The look in Ken's eyes, when he reached up, and slid them back into place, made her shiver. She reached up, caressing his forearm, moving her touch up to his shoulder. She stepped close, feeling bold now about taking custody of God's gifts, and plans. So she curved a hand around his neck, drawing him down, initiating a kiss that was open, mutually receptive, moist and warm.

They sighed in unison, a pleasured punctuation mark to what Kiara considered a distinct, treasured moment of homecoming.

Ken hadn't even thought about the bouquet. The fact that it was the first thing Kiara's attention fixed upon when she entered his home, however, left him keenly aware. Her focus on the item opened up his portion of some of the things that needed to be said between them, for the bouquet was a silk flower replica of the arrangement Kiara had given to Barb following Woodland's Autumn Fest years ago. In fact, it resided in the same low, expansive white wicker basket, at the center of Ken's living room coffee table.

Her eyes widened in instant recognition.

Ken tried not to feel sheepish and embarrassed; he tried to maintain balance when he had been caught in a gesture of a secret homage to Barb—and to Kiara.

Her gaze darted away from the now conspicuous display. In a shy, somewhat nervous gesture, she tucked a slice of hair behind her ear and moved inside.

Grace and poise back in place, she set her purse on the floor and sat down on the couch—but after a brief look into his eyes, she reached out to touch a rust colored mum.

"This is beautiful."

Her questioning glance left Ken, a wizened 30-something, at the precipice of a blush. But he was ready for the challenge now, and he gave her a nod, meeting her gaze head-on. "It honors two of the most spectacular women I've ever known." His voice went low. "But something tells me you already know that."

Kiara blew out a soft puff of air, and diverted her eyes. "When did you make this?"

"At the end of last year." Ken joined her on the couch. This time he was the one to reach out, and he stroked the petals of a vibrant, yellow bloom. "I finally felt ready to box up a few things, and donate them to charity. I came across the basket in a storage closet."

She listened intently, watching him. Ken continued. "Barb meant to do something with the basket, but—"

"But she died a month after my visit," Kiara murmured.

Ken nodded sadly. "She ran out of time." He sighed and scrubbed a hand across his face. Exploring the memory of Barb's last days wasn't the way he would have orchestrated this particular conversation, but things needed to be said, and understood, between him and Kiara. God would do the rest. So he simply let go and released himself into the moment.

"Time came, last fall, that I started to move forward," Ken said. "I packed things away and organized my life. I tried to go on."

"You did her proud."

Ken didn't agree or disagree. Instead, he *felt*; he embraced his emotions and strove to keep his voice from wavering. "I was boxing and sorting, wanting to finally, and fully, deal with the aftershocks of her death. That's when I found the basket." He paused.

Kiara nodded.

"It brought so many things to light. I remembered how your visit touched Barb—and me. How a simple, thoughtful gesture, in the form of a fall bouquet, lifted her spirits. It made me think about you. The effortless, instant way you touch people. It's an amazing gift, Kiara." He shrugged, wondering if anything he said made much sense. Judging by the soft, tender radiance of her eyes, she understood. "In that instant, in that moment of memory and perception, I woke up again. My heart, my focus, turned to you, and all the wonderful things that you are."

"So you recreated the bouquet."

"Symbolic—and safe enough a gesture to reemerging, I suppose, since it remained private. Until now."

Kiara shook her head, looking into his eyes with an expression he could only describe as amazement. "Ken, you never, ever fail to slide into my soul like a piece of velvet."

"What a coincidence," he replied, skimming a fingertip against the outline of her jaw, then her chin. "I could say the same thing to you."

A silence stretched between them before Ken picked up the conversational ball once more. "Love is about the process of surrendering just enough of yourself to say you want to grow in unison with someone else. It's not easy, but it's real, and it fills a part of your soul, and it lasts. If you let yourself find it and if you make that surrender it return."

"I think I understand that now. Better than I ever have," Kiara answered. "I don't control this, Ken. God does. *We* do. Give me the chance. Please? Have faith and let me follow His lead and be the person I want most to be. With you."

In the pause that followed Ken's heart stuttered, then began to pound.

"You've shown me possibilities. You've helped me remember how wonderful innocence is. I've been without that kind of purity for a long, long time. You helped me realize I haven't lost it for good. You showed me the way to a God who loves me, flaws and all. I suppose I thought I could hide those blemishes from the world at large. With God, with you. I can't. And what's more? I don't have to.

"I've worn armor all my life, of one sort or another. The right look, the right persona, the right way of life, but it wasn't truly me. It wasn't real. You saw through to the heart of me; then God entered in and did the rest. He transformed me into someone different. I thought you saw that end result. I thought you believed in my strength of conviction—my rebirth. If you need assurance, let me say this: I can't—I won't put on that armor ever again. It doesn't fit anymore. It doesn't protect me at all. It never did. I want to share who I am now, with you. But you need to make that step forward as well. You need to show me I matter, and that I have a place in God's plan for your life—if you think that's even the case."

He tucked her hands into his, looking straight and deep into her eyes when he whispered, "My turn now." He paused. "Kiara, nothing you do, nothing you've done is going to change what Christ did for you. You've been influenced by the people in your life, parents who pushed you past what they felt was a meager upbringing. Your beauty, internal and external, draws people in. Your personality warms hearts and opens them wide. Your taste for beauty, in all its forms is paramount to your job and the success you've found. You say you've made mistakes, veered off the path, let yourself be won over by glamour and material things. Name me one prophet who didn't stumble. Name one person who hasn't been tempted to do something they wouldn't ordinarily even consider."

"That's part of my point. You know my secrets, and my failings. What are yours?"

Ken shook his head. He focused on the bouquet for a moment, then on their joined hands. "The situation I've had to reason through and come to terms with is *you*, Kiara. And when I say that, I want you to take it very seriously. Don't brush it aside or ignore its impact on me. I want you to put yourself into the following scene and live it with me."

Ken focused on her intently. She watched, and waited.

"Over the past couple of years, as I got to know you, you pulled me in deeper and deeper. You enchanted me, Kiara." In an instant her face transformed from questioning to stormy. He hastened to add, "I mean that in the best possible way. Meanwhile, my wife, whom I loved beyond measure, the woman I pledged my whole life to, who possessed such beauty and such strength, began to fade. Her life dimmed as yours brightened. You filled me with vibrancy and laughter—with passion and hope. You brought me everything I most needed. I clung to every second I had with you, just as strongly as I held on to my wife as she died. Can you understand how guilty I felt? I never, ever imagined my life without her. I wanted my fifty or more years with her. I wanted a lifetime. I wanted kids, and grandkids, but that wasn't God's plan. I got angry with that at times. Anyone would. When I saw her suffering, it shattered me. I needed to find a way to deal with losing her, while at the same time, reconcile myself to the betrayal I felt in being so...so...*pulled* to you while Barb fought with every inch of her being to keep on living.

"Still, I met you and you entered my bloodstream. I haven't been the same since. I agonized over Barb. I watched her suffer and endure so much. I loved her. I *still* love her. But at the same time, I'd go to church, and I'd see you. Your vitality, your heart and your spirit—reached out and filled me up."

"I never knew. Not even for an instant—"

"How desperate I felt? How drawn I am to you?" he concluded for her.

Kiara nodded.

"Good. You weren't meant to. I hid as best I could. Then, when she died, I prayed for hours about what I felt was my heart betraying itself. That's when God provided me with the answer I sought."

"Which is?"

For emphasis he kept quiet, studying each curve and line of her face, saturating his needy heart with her beauty and soft tenderness of her jade colored eyes until he was certain he had her full focus. "He was preparing my heart, and my life, for *you*. It was Barb's time, but it wasn't *mine*. And God prepared me for you perfectly. He led you to my church where I got to know you, and understand the myriad of gifts you possess, the joy you give. No one prompted, no one pushed, you were *eager* to be part of the church. That passion made you part of my life in a very personal way. I let you in—couldn't help it. We worked side by side, and grew closer through every project we tackled. The church renovation. Working on church activities. The mission trip to Pennsylvania. You've become a partner, Kiara. Your spirit and love feeds mine. You're part of me now. No matter what's happened in either of our lives, Jesus' plan remains. That plan is *us*, Kiara. *Together*. And I promise you that we go forward together with every bit of love I have to give. It's yours. Forever."

EPILOGUE

Six Months Later

Sea waves tumbled and rumbled, a rhythmic punctuation that added life to the steamy, sun-drenched atmosphere that swept gradually through the interior of the hotel suite. Salt-tanged air swirled, tickling Kiara's senses alert, coming from the beach just beyond a set of wide open terrace doors.

Reluctantly she stirred, leaving slumber behind. She instantly found herself pulled backwards, drawn up tight against the long line of a strong, warm body. A low growl of approval came from the spot next to her in bed, as did a huskily spoken: "Good morning, Mrs. Lucerne."

She turned, sliding against Ken. She beamed when she came upon sleep-weighted, cocoa-colored eyes, a tumble of thick brown hair, and a smile of greeting that melted every bone in her body.

"Good morning," she replied, snuggling against him.

Ken lifted up to glance at the clock. "Unreal. It's already eleven o'clock in the morning? That's *not* possible. I'm completely losing track of time."

Kiara stroked her fingertips against the mild, abrasive stubble that shadowed his chin. "That's what the island of St. Thomas is for. Besides, sleeping in from time to time is a supreme indulgence and luxury. Don't knock it."

They drew together in a slow, rich kiss that went on and on and on and moved inexorably from lazy ease to fire and electricity. Kiara continued to melt, and she sighed, surrendering her all to the arms and heart of the man who rolled above her. He moved just far enough away to stroke back her hair, and study her eyes.

"Speaking of indulgence and luxury," he said, "we owe them."

"*Them* meaning Daveny and Collin."

Ken nodded.

Kiara giggled. "Yep. We sure do. They're experts at pampering."

A wooden ceiling fan spun lazily above them stirring air that already leaned toward pleasantly humid. Light increased, beaming chunky, thick rays that angled inward through the open doorway and the window above their bed. Sunshine glinted upon a band of yellow gold on the third finger of Kiara's left hand and her soul spun in a timeless dance of joy. Opting away from a traditional engagement ring and diamond, she told Ken what she wanted most were simple, matching wedding bands bearing a subtle, geometric design. Inside, both were inscribed: Ken & Kiara, April 3, United by God—in love.

Kiara's contentment lifted, growing until it was off the record charts. She studied the piece for, oh, about the millionth time since Ken had placed it on her finger during a candlelight ceremony held amidst a bevy of family and friends at Woodland Church just a few days ago.

Picking up the thread of their conversation, Kiara

continued. "I still can't believe they did this for us. I mean, all expenses paid? For a *week*? In the *Caribbean*?"

"Quite the honeymoon," Ken remarked huskily, his voice rough and sexy. When he nibbled on her neck, and shoulders, his warm breath gliding against her skin, Kiara went so brainless she nearly forgot what in the world they were talking about…

She murmured, through shivers, "All Daveny said is, *'I never had a sister, 'til I had you. You're my family. We just want you to enjoy it.'* I think we're fulfilling our part of the bargain."

Ken just laughed at that woeful understatement, continuing his nuzzling explorations. At present, he focused on her jaw. Next came the ticklish underside of her chin. Kiara closed her eyes, lifted to him, and sighed with delight.

"I'd have to agree with that assessment," he finally murmured.

They kissed once more and his flavor filled her; his textures and tastes blended with her own, becoming a whole unit—a spirit of one. Never had she experienced such pure and undiluted happiness.

Sliding way, Ken exclaimed, "Uh-oh…I almost forgot. I have a final wedding gift for my bride."

His bride. His. She'd never tire of that moniker. Kiara smiled with expectation, drawing the pale blue cotton sheet against her body as she sat up, and watched him root through his suitcase. From within he pulled out a small, soft-sided package wrapped in white and gold complete with a frilly wedding-esque bow. When he slipped back into bed and handed her the gift, Kiara just looked at him, knowing her happiness telegraphed straight through from her heart, to her eyes, to him. She nibbled on her lower lip, hiding an inner bout of laughter—because she had one last secret gift for him stashed away in her luggage as well.

Tearing into the wrapping, giving an appropriate 'Oooh' and 'Ahhh' to the packaging, she stopped short, silent and stunned when she saw what resided within the folds of paper.

It was a six pack of handkerchiefs, complete with monogram: *KAJL*

Kiara gaped, covering her trembling mouth. Obviously puzzled, Ken watched her. In confusion, he started to reach out, seeming to want to question her reaction, and perhaps reassure—but Kiara dashed out of bed before he could take hold of her hand, or get a word out. She tossed on a satin robe that was part of her wedding trousseau and made for her suitcase, moving fast to pull out a wrapped gift of her own that featured a small note card on top that was addressed to Ken.

Her husband.

The reality still caused her lips to tremble, her eyes to fill…

Wordless, she offered it to him—a smaller, soft-sided package quite similar to his.

Ken already smiled, pulling on her hand until she was back in bed with him. He sat up and propped his back against the headboard, watching her with teasing suspicion. "Is this what I think it is?"

Kiara couldn't hazard a reply. Her heart was too full, her throat too tight. A haze of tears blurred his image, but never, ever eradicated it completely. First, he opened and read the card. Then, his eyes went to smoke and silk, all things attractively, protectively, lovingly male… Message read, he looked into her eyes;

she was sure they sparkled with tears, and he simply nodded his agreement to the words she had inscribed within.

'Ken—my heart is yours. In happiness and in tears. All my love always—Kiara'

He pulled off wrapping paper, adding it to the pile that now decorated their puffy, down comforter of pale green. His smile spread fast and strong at what he found. "How appropriate," he murmured, watching Kiara slide a fingertip quickly beneath her eyes. Inside rested three handkerchiefs, complete with monogram: KJL

"I finally remembered to return them," she whispered, moved and overcome.

"So," Ken said, lifting up the one on top and holding it out to her. "Yours or mine?"

Kiara moved close and wrapped herself around him contentedly. In decision, she chose the top one from the package that had come from Ken—then accepted the one he offered as well—the one of his which she had just returned. "How about both?"

Ken laughed, and held her tight. "Sounds perfect to me, angel. Just perfect."

Be sure to look for the next books in the Woodland Church Series, Coming Soon!

Hearts Communion, Book 3

Jeremy "JB" Edwards dreams of one thing: Having a loving wife and children of his own. Not a surprising ambition, since he was raised at the heart of a large, tight-knit family.

Monica Kittelski spends her days at Sunny Horizons Daycare Center pouring her heart and faith into other people's children. But Monica harbors one impossible dream: Having children of her own someday.

JB and Monica seem the perfect match, but what will come of their electric, sassy relationship when Jeremy learns of Monica's infertility?

Hopes and reality collide when they must confront the idea of finding God's plan and following His will when a dearest hope is destined to remain unfulfilled.

Can these two loving, passionate hearts survive a communion of dreams and reality?

Hearts Key, Book 4

A chorus of faith sung in the key of second chances.

Life hasn't been as kind to Amy Maxwell. Once, the effervescent leader of the pack, her marriage should have been perfect. Instead, she escaped with nothing but the clothes on her back and her daughter, Pyper.

Tyler Brock is dazzling. The once shy teen has evolved into a powerhouse in Christian music, and when he returns to Woodland for a benefit concert, Amy can't believe he is as faithful and tender as ever. He even manages to touch the heart of a doubtful Pyper.

But, Amy can't escape her own self-doubt, and she questions the wisdom of her heart when it comes to the charismatic musician who is so different now, yet so much the same.

Can the key to their hearts unlock a lifetime of love?

**Haven't read the story that started it all?
Be sure to pick up Hearts Crossing,
Available now in electronic formats**

"How do you feel about God, Collin?"

"I don't."

Collin Edwards, a former parishioner at Woodland Church of Christ, has renounced God without apology, his faith drained away in the face of a tragic loss.

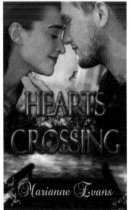

Daveny Montgomery cares deeply about her relationship with God and the community of Woodland. But lately she's been in a rut, longing for something to reignite her spiritual enthusiasm.

A beautification project at Woodland seems the answer for them both. Daveny spearheads the effort and Collin assists—but only with the renovations, and only because he wants to know Daveny better.

Despite his deepening feelings for her, even stepping into the common areas of the church stirs tension and anger.

Can Daveny trust in Collin's fledgling return to faith? And can Collin ever accept the fact that while he turned his back on God, God never turned his back on him?

Thank you for purchasing this White Rose Publishing title. For other inspirational stories of romance, please visit our on-line bookstore at www.whiterosepublishing.com.

For questions or more information contact us at info@whiterosepublishing.com.

White Rose Publishing
Where Faith is the Cornerstone of Love™
www.WhiteRosePublishing.com

May God's glory shine through this inspirational work of fiction.

AMDG